testosterone

testosterone

james robert baker

alyson books
los angeles | new york

ALL CHARACTERS IN THIS BOOK ARE FICTITIOUS. ANY RESEMBLANCE TO
REAL INDIVIDUALS—EITHER LIVING OR DEAD—IS STRICTLY COINCIDENTAL.

© 2000 BY RON ROBERTSON. ALL RIGHTS RESERVED.

MANUFACTURED IN THE UNITED STATES OF AMERICA.

THIS BOOK IS PUBLISHED BY ALYSON PUBLICATIONS,
P.O. BOX 4371, LOS ANGELES, CA 90078-4371.
DISTRIBUTION IN THE UNITED KINGDOM BY
TURNAROUND PUBLISHER SERVICES LTD.,
UNIT 3, OLYMPIA TRADING ESTATE, COBURG ROAD, WOOD GREEN,
LONDON N22 6TZ ENGLAND.

FIRST EDITION: OCTOBER 2000

00 01 02 03 04 **a** 10 9 8 7 6 5 4 3 2 1

ISBN 1-55583-567-8

LIBRARY OF CONGRESS CATALOGING-IN-PUBLICATION DATA
  BAKER, JAMES ROBERT.
    TESTOSTERONE / JAMES ROBERT BAKER.—1ST ED.
    ISBN 1-55583-567-8
      1. GAY MEN—FICTION. 2. MISSING PERSONS—FICTION. 3. LOS ANGELES
  (CALIF.)—FICTION. I. TITLE.
  PS3552.A4278 T4 2000
  813'.54—DC21   00-032769

A NOTE FROM THE EDITOR

Unfortunately, James Robert Baker passed away on November 5, 1997, and was therefore unable to oversee or even approve the final revisions to this wonderful novel. Consequently, in the final edit, I worked very hard to do as little as possible. Most of what I did was update cultural references, such as changing Baker's use of "AZT" to a more current AIDS treatment, "Crixivan," or, in one instance, "The Cocktail." I also changed the book's structure, though not the sequence. By that I mean that Baker originally broke the book into twenty-eight rather uneven (lengthwise) chapters. The breaks were fairly random, and the audio tapes—what I mean by "audio tapes" will become clear as you read the novel—are such a unique and interesting feature of this particular novel that it seemed far better, infinitely more natural, to break the text only at points where Dean Seagrave, the narrator-protagonist, changes tapes. (If anyone is interested, I did mark

A Note From the Editor

the original chapter breaks with a triple asterisk, an element that has been incorporated into the design of the book.) One further note: Square brackets were placed in the text by Baker—as annotations by him to Seagrave's words—not by me. I thought about adding a few of my own to explain some of Baker's more obscure cultural references, but decided against it. Part of the fun of reading Baker's work lies in sometimes having to guess to whom or what he's referring. If he were still alive, of course, I would have asked him to provide a few more annotations, and probably would have also asked him to delete a few that seemed, to me at least, unnecessary. Either way, this work, like all of Baker's books, is perfectly comprehensible even if you miss a few allusions.

I would like to thank James Robert Baker's life partner and literary executor, Ron Robertson, not only for giving me a chance to posthumously publish Baker's genius, but for working with me to ensure the final version is one of which James would have been proud.

For more information on James Robert Baker, log on to www.jamesrobertbaker.com.

Scott Brassart, Los Angeles

PREFACE

I don't really want to say a lot here; I think Dean Seagrave, in the transcript that follows, speaks very well for himself. I certainly don't want to proffer any sort of facile commentary on the difference between love and obsession. What I do want to say is that Dean represents to my mind a true tragedy.

I can't pretend to be objective. Dean was (and still is) a good friend. But even if I didn't know him, I would still have been bowled over by his artwork. His graphic novels—*Mean Beach, I Was a Queer for the FBI, Manson Girl Memories, Foto-Novella, I Was a Teenage Speed Freak*—are brilliant, funny, insanely inventive satiric works of the highest order. Despite his current circumstances, I hope he finds the will and the inspiration to draw again.

I can't condone Dean's actions or even offer an opinion on what Pablo Ortega did or did not *do* to him. I only met Pablo once, briefly, at an L.A. restaurant. He seemed pleasant

Preface

enough—and incredibly sexy in an oddly ineffable way.

It's an art world cliché, which many may understandably scoff at. But when I think of Dean Seagrave, the line that always comes to mind is: Genius and madness can be very close.

—James Robert Baker, Los Angeles

TAPE 1

Hey, Jim. By the time you hear this, I'll be dead. Just kidding. But you're probably wondering what this is. One thing it's not is what you were expecting: a tape of the Bad Religion show at the Palace. I missed that, as it turned out. A lot's been going on.

I'll tell what this is, on one level anyway. An experiment. A novel, a living novel, spoken directly onto tape. Without all the tedious typing and editing, and agents, publishers, printers, before the book-on-tape version. I'm skipping all that. And it's a living novel because it's taking place right now as I speak it. I mean, I don't know exactly what's going to happen. I don't know how each scene is going to unfold. But I do have a very rough sense of the narrative. I know the premise, you could say. I know the fundamental thrust of this thing. But I'm not going to spill it. I need to build my case first, so you don't think I've flipped out. In the meantime, I don't want to shoot too soon.

James Robert Baker

I'll tell you this much: I'm out looking for action, some very serious action, today. I'm seeking catharsis, a visceral catharsis—that's what I'm up to right now. I'm a no-bullshit guy, and one angry queer, so don't fuck with me because I'm on a mission. Attention all breeders: You'd better part for me like the Red fucking Sea, because I'm plenty pissed off, and if you get in my way, I'll ram your rear end and squash your little baby.

In fact, I'm in the car now, as you can no doubt tell. But if you're listening closely, you may already know that it's not my car. It's not my throaty '66 GTO. It's a Hertz rental car. A purposefully nondescript mouse-gray Nissan Maxima. At first they were going to give me a Sentra. Till I mentioned Nicole [Brown Simpson] and got a free upgrade.

I miss the power of my GTO. But I wrapped that around a sycamore almost two months ago. I wasn't drunk, in case you're wondering. I hadn't had a thing to drink, and I wasn't on drugs. I was spaced out and angry, I guess, and a few other things, maybe not paying attention. This happened on Old Canyon Road, on a stretch I know well. I mean, I know automatically where to slow down, but for some reason I didn't. Except it's not for *some reason*, like I don't know what the reason is. I know, I remember, exactly what I was thinking about when I drove off the road. I was thinking about Pablo Ortega. Remembering how much I liked to wrap my lips around his fat brown uncut cock. Then my lips became my car and his cock became the sycamore tree.

I broke the windshield with my head and got a pretty bad whiplash. Had to wear a brace for six weeks. That's why I still hadn't cleared the brush around my house, which I usually do in April. Not that it would have made any difference.

Except it would have made it more obvious the fire was set intentionally.

It happened in the middle of the night two weeks ago Thursday. I haven't been sleeping well; that's all that saved me. I tend to wake up a lot in the night. And sometimes I get up, smoke a cigarette to calm down again. Which is strange in that it's something that Pablo also does. So sometimes when I'd be doing that, smoking a cigarette in the dead of the night, I'd think about Pablo, doing the same thing at the same time somewhere else, thinking about me. So it gave me this strange sense of connection. Except that night he wasn't that far away. He wasn't across town somewhere, I'm convinced of that. I was smoking a cigarette in the bedroom, looking out at the moon through the eucalyptus trees, when I smelled the smoke downstairs. Saw the flames. I grabbed my pants; that was all. I saved nothing from the workroom. It was too late for that. It was three in the morning, so nobody saw the flames or called. By the time I got to the first yuppie house on Saddle Peak Road and woke them up, my house was completely engulfed in flames. Five units arrived within twenty minutes. But there was nothing left to save.

The fire inspector said a cigarette started it. Someone flicked a cigarette from a car. He tried to blame me for not clearing the brush. Like it was an accident. Carelessness, that is, instead of deliberate arson. I argued with him about this, but he kept insisting it wasn't arson. He got defensive, like I was questioning his expertise. I asked what the cigarette brand was—if he'd said Kools, that would've cinched it—but he wouldn't tell me. I let it go at that point. I didn't need evidence. I already knew what I was going to do. I was going to kill Pablo. I'd known that for several weeks before the fire. The fire just convinced me that if I didn't kill him, he'd kill me. He'd just tried.

I tried to minimize the impact of the fire in my mind. Most of what was lost, the original artwork, was in a sense sentimental. Most of it's been published. It's out there, it still exists in the world. So it was like losing the original cels of *Fantasia* or something when dozens of prints are still in distribution. I kept using that analogy so I wouldn't feel raped and buttfucked and lobotomized. But I think that finally I was beyond a certain kind of anger. Which is good. It's given me clarity, resolve. To just do what needs to be done.

A man's gotta do what a man's gotta do. I can never remember who said that. Clint Eastwood? Liberace? Margaret Thatcher? Maybe all three.

I've been staying at Charlie's, sleeping on the sofa. He's back in New York now. I've had the place to myself for the last three days. Which has been good. It's given me a chance to prepare for today. Without sneaking around. Or having Charlie try to talk me out of it.

In a way, I'm still numb. About the fire, I mean. I keep thinking of things that were lost. Specific books. The books— that's the main thing I can't replace. Fifteen years of books, many out of print now. That's where it starts to feel like a lobotomy. But the main loss, the crucial loss, was my new work in progress. Which was actually almost finished. My new *graphic novel,* even though I hate that term now, *Testosterone.* Which I think, which I know, was the best thing I've done so far. By far, the most autobiographical. I don't like to think of art as therapy, as you know. I mean, that's insulting, condescending. And irritating because it's not completely untrue. And *Testosterone* was, in a certain respect, a kind of "working out" of feelings about things that happened with Pablo. Not that it was literal. I don't like these terms like "surreal" or "magical realism." But I would say "magical paranoia." That's the term that occurred to me at one point, though I'd never use it in an interview. I wouldn't want to be stuck with it or have to explain what it meant. But it felt right as a description of the mood I was trying to create and, in fact, created. I've tried telling myself that: that I did the work, I performed the exorcism, and that it can't be undone even though the work itself is lost. But here's the problem: It feels undone. Or as if, perhaps, it was always an incomplete exorcism, a failed exorcism. Which I think in a sense it was. Because this story of evil magic has been incredibly ongoing. I mean, even though Pablo and I "broke up" over a year ago, new information keeps coming to light, new curses, new spells. I keep finding little hex packets hidden in my psyche, and this was going on even as I drew *Testosterone*. Some of this new material I worked in as I went. But at a certain point you have to freeze things, you have to say "Enough." Except the Pablo material wouldn't stay put. It kept growing like a lethal virus creeping over the edge of the petri dish. So even as I finished *Testosterone* and savored a sense of *artistic* accomplishment, I knew that in another very real and important way, it was already spiritually dated.

I'm on PCH right now, incidentally, heading north toward the Malibu. I don't know why I just said that—*the* Malibu— except it sounds pretentious, affected, and that amuses me, and I need some amusement right now. But here's the real point. I'm passing the Tuna Canyon turnoff...right now. So there's a kind of geo-verbal synchronicity in my telling you about the burning love house now. That's how I think of it. I think of that X song. Do you remember that X song, "Burning House of Love"? That was Pablo's favorite group from his teenage years. He was nostalgic about it. He had memories. Just like Sean Young in *Blade Runner*. Music, I think, was our one meeting ground, besides sex. But in that song, if you remember, John Doe is obsessed. He's broken up with Exene or something, and she's got a new boyfriend and he's jealous, and he talks about going for a drive to "burn your love house down." It's a good song. I'm nostalgic for it. For the time when it made sense. When I was just obsessed.

It's funny. Pablo had to drive this way a lot. On the way out to see his new boyfriend or victim. Which is where I'm going right now. Out to Decker Canyon, to see this poor sucker Brice. So all the time I was looking for him in all these other strange parts of L.A., he was still over here on the Westside. He was still on this highway. So it would've been convenient for him to start the fire.

I know he did it. Payback for what I did to his mother. In a way it's still jolting, though. I expected a reaction when I roughed up his mother. That's why I did it. To smoke him out. But I didn't expect him to burn my house down in the dead of night, to try and kill me. It's crazy, but I didn't expect *him* to want to kill *me*. That's left over from the period where he was the coolly rational figure and I was cast in the role of spurned psycho. That was the first thing he did to me.

That's one of the things that still pisses me off. The idea that *anyone* did something to me, let alone this stupid beaner with no sense of humor. I'm just not into being a victim. I'm not a masochist. Maybe he thought I was. Except I'd rather think I was just trusting. I'd hate to think that it all boils down to sadists and victims. But one of the things Pablo did to me is he's got me thinking that way.

He's not stupid, incidentally. I probably already mentioned that. I know the version you got of the whole thing was sketchy. Dean has a new boyfriend, they're in love, it's intense, then they fight, have some problems, break up. Something like that. The official summarized version. But I know I'd often emphasize his intelligence as a kind of reassurance to my fellow Anglo friends. Like: He's Latino, but he doesn't have an accent (like your typical dumb beaner). Born in refined, Eurocentric Chile (not cruddy scumbucket Mexico), but a U.S. citizen. And above all a doctor, a brilliant research scientist. Later, after we "broke up," when I talked about his lack of humor, his inability to laugh, I'd say: "It's not that he wasn't intelligent, he was very intelligent...." Which is true. He was, is. He's also a ghoul and a sadist. But here's the thing, here's the sick part. He thinks that's cool. He's a kind of guy who'd be hard to insult that way. If you called him a vampire, he'd take it as a compliment. He'd say, "I warned you," and then he'd work in the term "emotional serial killer." That was the actual warning. He didn't say, "I'm an emotional serial killer." It was slightly more oblique. What he said was, "Calvin," this odious queen best friend of his, "Calvin attracts emotional serial killers, and he thinks I might be one too. But we had this big talk about it, and I convinced him I'm not. That when I break up with someone, I always explain why it's not working out. I don't just dump them brutally the way these guys always dump Calvin." It was something like that, those aren't the exact words. But at this point we'd been going together for maybe a month and I felt smug. I mean, I felt like it was working, I didn't see it as a warning, even when he said, "Be careful, watch out." I mean, he actually said that. But it seemed weirdly charming or antic or something, like he was striking this ironic "dangerous" pose. Which is an odd thing about Pablo. He could strike these strange poses that I secretly thought of as woefully ridiculous. The equivalent of Maria Montez saying, "I know many men say I am cruel." Not that Pablo talks like she does with a campy accent. He has his own pose-defeating speech pattern, which in his case evokes a very unexotic image of a Latino youth in flared jeans watching Suzi Quatro on *Happy Days* circa 1974 in a middle-class house in Granada Hills. That Roseanne thing, although a lot of people do it now: Saying *goes* instead of *said*. "So Calvin goes, 'Pablo, guys just realize you're someone worth having...' And I go: 'Calvin...'" Which kind of drives me up the wall in a way. Because it sounds stupid, it *sounds* lowlife and Valley. Of course, I'm six years older than Pablo, part of the last generation that still says *said*.

Another time he struck a pose like that, with this riff in a restaurant, this Casanova love-god riff. "When guys look at me," he said across the table, "they think of one thing: sex." I laughed, which pissed him off. He said, "What are you laughing at?" I don't remember what I said, but I didn't say, "You." I didn't say that, but I got the point across. Except I wasn't laughing at him in some mean, put-down way. God knows, I thought of sex when I looked at him. I just wanted us to laugh. Which, with Pablo, was wanting the impossible.

I mean, he *couldn't* laugh. He couldn't, in the same way that mutes can't talk. I noticed this early on, of course, and he commented on it before I could. Like he was aware that he never laughed, but he didn't really offer an explanation. I just accepted it at first as an odd personality tic. And to be blunt, it didn't really matter a whole lot when the fucking was as good as it was. But it was strange, and it seems strange now, since humor is so important to me, since I'm essentially a satirist, that I'd get involved with someone who never laughed at all.

Except he did once, actually. Just once. At a trailer for some piece-of-shit Bette Midler movie. We'd gone to the New Beverly to see *The Long Goodbye,* and even before the trailers we'd been sitting there discussing different films. This was pretty early in our relationship, and just from talking about different films, I'd started to feel somewhat disturbed, since everything I liked Pablo hated and vice versa. So I guessed correctly that he wasn't going to care for *The Long Goodbye,* which is one of my all-time favorite films. But I was thinking: Hey, it would be dull if everyone agreed. And anyway, who cares when the fucking's so good? And then this trailer came on for that total dog of a movie with Bette Midler and Woody Allen, the one where he carries the surfboard around the shopping mall—I'm blocking the title—and suddenly, with zero warning, Pablo let out this quick but hideous wet shriek. I mean, a *shriek,* which to me is not sexy. *Queens* shriek, queens shriek at Bette Midler movies. But Pablo's not a queen. He doesn't act or speak at all effeminately. Not that he's off at the other extreme into some hard posturing machismo number. He just has this kind of natural, maybe jocklike masculine demeanor, so this shriek came as a real shock. And I kind of thought: Well, if that's what his laugh sounds like, maybe it's just as well...

But here's another explanation, one this therapist I was seeing for a while thought of. Bob, this psychologist. With long silver hair. Actually, he looked a lot like *Twin Peaks* Bob. You kept expecting him to hop over the couch or something. But Bob said, when I mentioned Pablo's inability to laugh, "Was there anything wrong with his teeth?" And suddenly it hit me: Yes, I think Pablo's front teeth may be slightly crooked. Not in a way that I ever noticed that much, or that anyone would find objectionable, but maybe he was self-conscious about it. It was dark in the movie theater the one time he cut loose. I don't know what the point is, but I forgave Pablo a lot. I mean, physically. He wasn't perfect, but who is? Still, I may have transformed him because the sex was so good. Or because I was in love with him.

Which is not to say that he isn't hot. It's kind of true that when you look at him, it's hard not to think of sex. His body is *OK*. I mean by that he's not all built up, which I find repulsive anyway, that muscle-queen look. He's got a good body is what I'm saying. And a really hot face. Except it seems weird, even now, to reduce him to the physical. To say, hot bod, nice butt, juicy uncut cock, hot face, like Andy Garcia. Even if it's true, which it is.

Andy Garcia. He can play Pablo when this becomes a big Hollywood movie. Of course, I'll be played by William Petersen. *Eight Million Ways to Live and Die in L.A.*

Andy Garcia was a big reference point in *Testosterone*. In one section especially, that was drawn from *Internal Affairs*. I was the Richard Gere character there. But instead of beating Andy up in an elevator, I fucked him. Instead of telling him I fucked his wife in the ass, I fucked him in the ass. Instead of his wife going crazy, he did. That was a strange film, though. This twisted competition between two guys who should've been fucking. Kind of like this is now.

It's difficult, I think, with two male-identified men. It might have been a lot easier if Pablo had been a cha-cha boy, a little mambo queen. But he looked like Andy Garcia with a beatnik goatee. Which is strange, that's become such a massive cliché now. Goatees. I don't know if Pablo was a trendsetter or if it came out of an older Latino tradition. Like a *cholo* goatee. Or if it's all part of the same thing now, since all this Latino stuff is really in. But to me, at the time, the goatee signified "bohemian."

At first, the first night we met, I didn't realize he was Latino. I mean, it was dark, I couldn't see him that well, and the first label I put on him was "student". Since he said he was taking a break from working on his paper. He looked like a student, black Levi's, faded Concrete Blonde T-shirt. This was at the beach in Ocean Park, the cruising beach. Most people don't know that's where I met him. After we were going together, once we'd become boyfriends, I didn't feel like telling people we met at a sleazy pickup spot and went back to his place for sex like cheap tricks. So I'd say we met through friends at a party or something. I don't know why now I felt embarrassed, exactly. It's not like my friends are that prissy, with one or two exceptions. I guess I just didn't want people leering or smirking.

But that's where it happened. At the beach, which was

strange. Because I hadn't gone down there much for years. I mean, back in the seventies, the early eighties, I used to. When I lived in Venice I'd go down there a lot. I'd walk down there at night, fool around, get sucked off. Stop at Muni's Liquor on my way home, snag a pint of Häagen-Dazs. That's not *all* I did in those days. I had boyfriends, fuck buddies, sex-and-dinner dates, a wife and kids at one point—just kidding. But it was one of the things I did a lot.

Then I moved out of Venice in '84, moved up the coast to Tuna Canyon, became this hermit. I mean, I still had my friends, like you, but I went through some really long periods of celibacy. I don't talk about this a lot. It makes people too crazy. Gay people, I mean. Gay men. Especially in those days, in the mid eighties, I learned to keep my mouth shut. There was so much hysteria, denial: *I'm not going to stop having sex.* How many times did I hear people say that, essentially out of the blue? Not that I'd suggested they should. I didn't care what other people did. If they wanted to go out and eat twenty strange butts a night, my feeling was: Hey, bon appetit. But for me, for a long time, the idea of actual sex, as opposed to jack-off fantasies, seemed contaminated.

But know what? That period really bores me now—the empty years, I mean—so I'm not going to bore you by doing "Confessions of a Celibate." The whole point is, I went for a long time without getting much—out of choice. And I'm not really sorry now, since that may be why I'm negative. That, in fact, is the one good thing that's happened in the last year. Finally taking the test and coming up negative. Not that it's changed as much as I thought it would.

But here's the real point. Right before I met Pablo, I'd been rediscovering sex. I mean, there'd been the thing with Rich the year before. He seems really hapless and well-intentioned now, incidentally. But after that blew up, I started hitting different cruising spots. The park a few times, but mostly the beach. Like a safe-sex version of the old days. Jack-off scenes. And, to be honest, a few times I let guys blow me, though not to the point of coming, and I wouldn't blow them. I was still playing this game where I thought most of the time: I probably don't have it. Which was good in a way, as it turned out, since I didn't.

But I was starting to feel that I was maybe getting readdicted to anonymous sex. I mean, during the celibate period I liked to think that I was on a kind of fast. I saw myself as damaged, or emotionally shut down, from all the anonymous sex of the pre-AIDS era. So I thought by being celibate I was putting some distance between myself and all that, somehow "getting ready" for something more meaningful. So when I started going to the beach again, I saw myself slipping back, regressing. So when I met Pablo and that started up and looked serious and we agreed to be monogamous, I had this great sense of relief that I'd been saved from the now-deadly patterns of the past.

He said he was negative. While we were talking there that first night at the beach, before we went back to his place. He'd invited me, I guess, and I was hesitating. Thinking that I kind of just wanted to get sucked off at the beach, no muss, no fuss. That's the truth of it. He said, "I don't want to twist your arm." Then I said something about only being into safe things. That's when he said he'd just tested negative.

For some reason that unlocked my libido. When we got

back to his place, I mean. This place in Venice where he was house-sitting. He started blowing me and I blew him. And I wasn't afraid, since I knew he was negative. Rich and I never blew each other, since he also hadn't taken the test.

So for the first time in ten years I wasn't terrified on some level. Pablo was blowing me, but he didn't seem that worried. I liked that too, his attitude. The fact that he really liked sex. I felt like: OK, finally, I can relax and do what I've wanted to do for the last ten years. Because I really like sex too. I like a nice juicy cock in my mouth as much as the next man, especially when you don't have to worry about death. And most of all, more than anything, I love to fuck butt. Pablo claimed the first night that he didn't like to get fucked. But he did. He just wasn't going to give me everything right away.

It's funny. That first night at the beach, Pablo approached *me*. Which I thought about later when *Twin Peaks* Bob said, "Vampires always make the first move." Said this without knowing how or where I met Pablo, since I censored that. Didn't want to "explain" gay cruising to Bob. But that's how it happened. I'd seen Pablo get out of this Saab he was driving and go over and sit down on the grass. It was actually this park, this small park, by the beach. He asked me once later if I would've approached him. Like he wanted to know my first impression, if I'd been attracted to him. I told him the truth, kind of, that I probably wouldn't have, that something about him intimidated me. He had this air of easy self-assurance that made me feel nervous in comparison, and the Saab had stuck-up yuppie connotations. But the real truth is that even when we talked I wasn't that attracted to him. He was good-looking, but he didn't really *galvanize* me. He wasn't somebody I had to have or else. But once we had sex I was hooked. And the more we did it, the more hooked I got.

It could have been just a one-night stand. I'm still not sure why it wasn't. But after we had sex we talked for a while. He asked me what I did and when I told him, he said, "Oh, right. My friend Calvin is really into all that." Meaning comic books, graphic novels, 'zines. He mentioned another friend of his, a Cal Arts graduate, an ex-boyfriend who was an artist. This turned out to be Mark Spivey. But he made it sound like he knew a lot of artists and art world people, even though he himself was a scientist. He was vague on that point. He mentioned Cal Tech in a way that that made it sound like he taught there or did research there but had taken a sabbatical to write a major research paper. He had a part-time job with the county, he said, but he wasn't specific. He was house-sitting in Venice, he said, because his apartment building in the Wilshire District was being renovated and the noise made it hard for him to work there. I asked him what his research paper was about, and he said, "Well, it's pretty technical. But it has to do with the way HIV affects the brain." He talked about it in more detail until I saw that he was right, it was essentially beyond me in terms of neurobiological jargon.

But I liked the idea that he was a scientist, instead of another artist or a writer, or some kind of volatile, paranoid creative person, like Rich. Or me. I thought of Janice, who was always having these fucked-up affairs with other artists, who'd get crazy and competitive and all that. Until she finally settled down with an astronomer. I saw Pablo and me as a similar case of opposites complementing each other.

Pablo seemed like a scientist. I mean, his personality, that kind of dry intelligence. What I see now is that Pablo is by far more WASP than I am. Which I think is intentional. As if to succeed in the Anglo science world he's cultivated this cool, dispassionate approach. While I'm just the opposite. Having come from this tight-assed WASP Republican background, I've tried to be more like the stereotype of Latins. Spontaneous, expressive: Get those emotions out. So it's strange because with Pablo all those stereotypes were reversed. I was the volatile hothead, he was the cool customer. Which is not to say he doesn't have a temper. He just knows how to hold it in. It took me a while to see this for some reason. I think his brown skin fooled me at first, so I didn't realize how much he was really like my father.

I'm passing Zuma Beach now. It's not much farther. Brice is up on Decker Canyon Road. He's not expecting me, but I think he'll still be there. I called right before I left Charlie's. When he answered, I hung up. He's embarrassed, and I don't blame him.

See, this is what happened. I ran into Pablo and Brice about three months ago at El Coyote, and I lost it. I was there with Charlie. We were going to a movie. Charlie's been a great friend though all this, incidentally. So we were just leaving and Pablo and Brice were coming in, and at first I wasn't sure it was him. I mean, my mind's been doing this number on all these different guys with goatees now, which has been driving me crazy, since I'm constantly seeing guys who look at first glance like Pablo. Then I saw the hairline scar over his eyebrow and knew it was him. I had half a second where I could've just kept walking, but I knew I'd be a pussy for the rest of my life if I did. So I blew and tried to grab Pablo. I said,

"You fucking piece of slime." But Pablo jumped back and then Charlie grabbed me. So then I said to this Brice guy, who kind of looks like an innocent-eyed young Keith Carradine, "Run!" I actually said this. I said, "Run for your life! This guy's a fucking vampire. He'll suck your heart out of your throat."

Pablo said, "You need help." Which completely set me off again. Since that's the whole way he's tried to position me, like I'm the one with the problem.

So I said, "What I need is your fucking head in a box of ice, motherfucker!" Which comes from *Testosterone*, this allusion to *Bring Me the Head of Alfredo Garcia*, which I knew that he got, since he knows I have a thing about that film—even though he's only into Bette Midler movies or those crappy South American films based on Gabriel Garcia Marquez stories.

That was basically it. The manager was coming over, and Charlie pulled me out the door, but I remember Brice's wide-eyed horrified look, no doubt wondering on some level if he should heed my warning. So I kind of wished I'd been less over-the-top and psycho and therefore easy to dismiss since, believe it or not, I really was thinking of Brice.

So Charlie got me out to the car and we left, even though at that point I'd been looking for Pablo for months. But my conscious intention had just been to *talk* to him, to get some sense of closure, to at least get some clue as to what had happened from his side. And obviously that had been blown, so it seemed right to go. But later I kicked myself, that Charlie had been there, that I'd missed my chance to smash Pablo's fucking face through the plate glass window.

Then, about a week before my house burned down, I got this message from Brice on my machine. He sounded very drunk, and he said, "I just want you to know you were right about Pablo. I should've listened. He made me think you were crazy, but I don't think you are now. I'm really sorry I didn't listen. I think I know what you're going through."

He also said his name, just his first name, but he didn't leave a number. So it took me a while to find out his last name and look up the number. But when I called him back, he claimed he couldn't remember calling me, which is possibly true. Then he shut down, blew me off, which I can understand, since I might be the one person who knows how badly he got hurt. A part of me doesn't want to disturb him. But if certain people are right about certain things, he may be in a lot more danger than he knows.

OK, I'm coming to Decker Canyon now. It's coming up here pretty quick. I'm curious in a way to see how it happened. How Pablo dumped him. It seems to happen different ways. Like he tailors it to the individual for maximum cruelty and long-term devastation.

Here's how he did it to me. It was a Friday night at my place in Tuna Canyon. Pablo was going to spend the weekend. We'd just eaten dinner. We were going to watch *Tie Me Up! Tie Me Down!* But first we were lying on the bed, still dressed, but kind of making out. The part I always remember is how he had a hard-on. Even though he knew just what he was going to do. Which was this. He suddenly rolled back and said, "Shit. I forgot to stop and get cigarettes." Which of course was a drag, since it's a six-mile drive down to the liquor store. But he sits up and starts pulling on his shoes.

So I decide to do some more work while he's gone. Figuring he'll be gone about a half hour. I get caught up in what I'm doing, and the next thing I know it's an hour later. So I'm worried for a second, since you know what the road is like. Except then I notice that his knapsack isn't there, which he always brings when he stays over. I realize that tonight he never brought it in.

So I have this feeling, even though we've been getting along. I mean, we had some strange fights, which I'll get into later, but at this point nothing seems to be wrong. But on a hunch I call his number in Venice. I can't believe it, but the phone's been disconnected. So that's when I know what's up. Except I still can't quite believe it. I think maybe I'm being paranoid, so I drive down to the liquor store on PCH. He could've had car trouble. But of course he's not there. So I drive to the house in Venice, this bungalow on Rialto. The house is dark. But I can look in the windows, since the curtains have been taken down, and see that it's empty. I drove back by a week or so later and found out the guy he'd supposedly been house-sitting for was not in Europe but had actually died of AIDS. Pablo was just doing some realtor a favor. I called his work number at the Medical Examiner's Office downtown and got a secretary who told me he no longer worked there. She claimed not to know where he was, and when I asked why he'd quit, she said, "I'm not at liberty to discuss the circumstances of Dr. Ortega's termination." So I didn't know what the fuck was going on. I tried to reach him at Cal Tech, where he'd supposedly been researching this paper he was writing. But I struck out completely there.

Since then I've gone through about a thousand different emotions, but for a long time I was just in shock. I mean, naturally I tried to figure out what I'd done, since clearly he was mad at me. Like he'd been mad at me for a while but kept it to himself. Knowing he was going to be leaving the place in Venice on a certain date, maybe he'd figured it was easier to disappear than have a big breaking-up scene, which admittedly could have become heated. Like I say, we did have some fights. I don't mean I ever hit him, or that he ever hit me. They weren't physical fights in that sense, except we kind of wrestled a few times.

The first time anything like that happened was at this restaurant, this Spanish place in Santa Monica, where he threw a glass of water in my face and I flipped and chased him outside and up the alley, where I grabbed him against a chain-link fence and fucked him in the ass. I mean, that's what happened. I yanked down his jeans and spit in my hand to lubricate my cock and fucked him in the ass without a rubber. The first time I'd done that in years. Fucked some guy raw in the butt without a rubber. So I mean, it put me away. His butt was so tight and spit is not the best lubricant, so I felt like I was tearing him up, and I liked it. I liked it a lot, and so did he. He was going crazy, groaning in pain/pleasure. And it was all I could do to pull out before I came, but I did. Even though it kind of freaked me out later, realizing he wouldn't have cared if I'd come up his ass, even though he didn't know my status.

Fuck, this is crazy. I'm getting a hard-on right now, just remembering that night.

But the point is this. Yes, there was a point. That's basically what our fights, what all our fights, were like. We'd always ended up fucking. Which disturbed me initially, then I didn't care. The truth is, there's a part of me that would still like to fuck Pablo again right now today. I can still run this fantasy, which I ran for a long time, that I'd find him and we'd have this big fight but end up fucking. I really wish like anything it could be like that, but I don't have access to that kind of magic. I know too much now and there's no going back. The sex part of our relationship is over.

I'm on Decker Road now, incidentally. This is a strange area. Dry brush, a few scattered houses here and there. You know who else lives up here? John Lilly. You have to be a weirdo to live up here. It's very remote. I'm looking for the address now. On the mailboxes. Fourteen, fifteen. OK, this must be it. Hmm. Strange. OK, I'm stopping here. There's a dirt road leading back to a trailer in some eucalyptus trees. An old Peugeot out front. I guess Brice is home. OK, here I am. I wonder if he's seen me yet. This is sad, man. I see myself in this guy. This whole hermit trip. I guess Pablo likes them vulnerable.

OK, I'll be back in a while. Or maybe real soon if he freaks out. That's why I'm not taking the Walkman. I should, but I'm not callous enough to play sleazebag reporter and surreptitiously record him. I'm being invasive enough as it is.

❊ ❊ ❊

OK, I'm back. Let me get out of here, in case he's watching from the window. Don't want him to think I'm talking to myself. Not that it matters. He still thinks I'm crazy. Let me turn around here in John Lilly's driveway. There's a dolphin on the mailbox. Must be his place.

So anyway. That was an odd scene. Poor fucking guy. He's hurting. I mean, he's one lonesome cowboy. Which is what he is, I think. A literal cowboy. OK, maybe a ranch hand. He does something like that up around here somewhere, with horses. He's from Arizona. Tucson, I think. He's not stupid, though. I'll tell you what he is. He's a fucking doll. Sandy hair, blue eyes. Shit, I'm starting to sound like some old auntie. It's true though. He triggered something from my distant past. Like from when I was twenty and trying to be straight but still getting crushes on different guys. Not that I was tempted to relive the past. Even though at one point I had a chance to.

So at first I had this kind of creepy feeling. Walking up to the trailer, where the door's standing open. There's this dry wind blowing, rustling the eucalyptus trees. A serious *Chinatown* feeling. Like I'm going to find this ineffably beautiful young man in there with flies buzzing over him, his wrists slit or something. Then I see him standing in the door in his underwear, eating a burrito. He's taller than I remembered from El Coyote, bigger. He freezes with a mouthful of beans.

I say, "Hi, look. I don't want to bother you, but I really need to talk to you."

I can see that he recognizes me. He swallows and says, "Yeah, OK. I had a feeling you'd track me down eventually."

So I go into the trailer and we sit at the table, this yellow formica table, and he offers me a drink of Jack Daniel's, which I accept. He adds some to the Coke he's drinking with his burrito. He looks like he drank most of the bottle the night before. He's still in his Jockey shorts. The way he's sitting, leaning back with one foot up on his seat, I can see his crotch, the shape of his dick. I know that he knows this. I try to stay focused on his eyes, his face. He's growing a goatee.

He says, "Pablo showed me one of your comic books. The

one about speed freaks. *I Was a Teenage Speed Freak.*" He forces a smile. "Funny but strange."

I say, "Yeah, I know. So what else did Pablo tell you about me?"

He looks at me. "Do you really want to hear all that?"

I say, "He told you I was crazy, right?"

He says, "Yeah, he said that. He said it started out OK, then you got possessive."

"Did he say how it ended?"

Brice nods.

I say, "What did he tell you?"

"He said he tried to end it cleanly, but you flipped out. He said you kept calling him, threatening to kill yourself if he didn't come back to you."

Well, this seriously pisses me off. I mean, I feel myself going into this rage state, with the heartbeat, adrenaline, the whole bit. And I really don't want to get into that yet. I'm going to need all that later. I don't want to burn up all my fuel sitting in a trailer. So I just say, "That's not how it happened," as calmly as I can. And tell him how it happened, how Pablo stepped out for cigarettes.

He kinds of smiles and pours himself a straight shot and says, "Well, at least you were still mo-*bile,* pardner." He doesn't talk with a twang, incidentally. But he uses corny phrases that kind of indicate his background.

I ask him what he means about mobility. And he smiles and says kind of sheepishly, "Well, you know, we got into some stuff."

I say, no, I don't know, what stuff?

He says, "Well, you know. With rope. He liked to be tied up. I guess you know that, though, right? You guys musta done that too, right?"

I say, "Not really." And I already feel this kind of weird sick envy. Since for some reason, I used to have *thoughts* about tying up Pablo. I mean, it's the kind of stray fantasy I've had, which I've never really done, of tying some guy up and fucking him. And I thought about it with Pablo, but I never really brought it up. So for a second I have this crazy idea that maybe if I *had* done that, if *we'd* gotten into that, I could've kept him. Like maybe he'd just been getting sexually bored. Except obviously that wasn't true, since he'd gotten into that with Brice and dumped him anyway.

I feel like I'm entering a kind of creepily vicarious or voyeuristic mode, but I still have to ask: "So what do you mean? You'd tie him to the bed?"

"Oh, no. He liked it standing up." Brice looks out the window. "Right out there. To the tree. He liked to be raped. Man, he'd go crazy. You can still see his come stains all over the tree bark. Christ Almighty, I sure loved to watch that big evil uncut dick of his shoot."

"I know," I tell him. "The next best thing to watching them fire that big fucking cannon they lugged across Spain in *The Pride and the Passion*." I know he won't get the reference. He's too young, and it's too obscure. But I get it.

He says, "Well, who am I trying to kid? The sex was a factor. Didn't have much else in common. Guess you know how that is. Man oh man, did he love to get fucked."

I'm trying not to notice that he's getting a hard-on. "So you just tied *him* up?"

"Oh, no, man. No, he liked to switch off. He liked to tie my hands behind my back and push me down to my knees. Wave that big brown dick in my face, make me beg for it. You know."

"Right."

"It was strange at first," he says. "Before Pablo, I'd always been pretty vanilla. That scares me sometimes."

"What do you mean?"

Suddenly, he gets up and says, "Damn, I forgot my medication."

For a second I kind of shit, thinking it's going to be Crixivan or AZT or something. But he gets this pill bottle—and I'm trying not to notice this semierection in his Jockey shorts—and as he takes out a capsule, he says, "Prozac, man. For my depression. I hope all that shit they say isn't true. Don't want to flip out and kill a bunch of people."

He tosses the pill back with a hit of Jack D.

"So were you guys having safe sex?" I say.

He shrugs and sits down again. "No need to. Both negative."

Another threadbare illusion bites the dust. Even though I know all about Pablo now, I'd still wanted to believe the unsafe sex we had, the unrubberized fucking, was somehow unique to us and special.

I say, "So what is it that you're scared about?"

He says, "What do you mean?"

I say, "You said you were scared."

He says, "I don't remember that. I'm not scared. I'm not scared of anything. I'm fearless."

He's getting drunk. And I get this sense that he's a violent drunk. So I'm running out of time. I say, "So what happened? How did you guys finally break up?"

He says, "Break up? Who says we broke up?"

I say, "Well, *you* did, I guess. In your message on my machine." But for a second I'm confused, wondering if in fact they've made up, if they're seeing each other again.

He pours another drink, offers me one, which I accept. My second, his sixth. He says, "I'll tell you what happened. We drove up to this ranch in Agoura. A place my boss—my *ex*-boss—owns. The place was for sale, nobody around. Barn, stables, corral. This was a Saturday, hot. He tied me to a fence post. Right out in the sun. I was sweating. Then he tore off my shirt, pants, pulled off my boots, everything. Stripped me bare. Rougher than he'd ever been, not that I minded. Then he fucked me, fucked me good. The next thing I knew, I heard the car starting up. Then I was eatin' dust. I thought at first it was part of the game. A new wrinkle. But he didn't come back. Not that day, not that night, not the next day. He'd tied the ropes tight. I couldn't get loose. The boss came by on Monday, with some real estate people, a woman in a blue dress. By then I'd pissed and shit all down my legs. So he fired me. But here's the part that makes me feel like I'm sick: The only part I didn't like was the sunburn."

So I'm kind of dazed and kind of appalled. And completely caught off-guard when suddenly, without warning, he starts to cry. These big, wrenching, chest-heaving sobs. He covers his face with his hands. I think about comforting him, but I get this sense that if I touch him, he'll turn violent. I mean, this guy's really schizzy. I know it's time to go, so I say, "Look, I really need to talk to Pablo. I'm not mad at him anymore, I just need to clarify things. I need a sense of closure. Can you tell me where he is?"

He wipes tears from his face and says, "I don't know where he is. But if I did, I wouldn't tell you. I know what kinda closure you got in mind."

I say, "No, really. I'm not mad anymore. That's the point. I think it would be good for both of us if we have a moment of mutual forgiveness."

He says, "Man, don't try and bullshit me. I can see what you're up to in your eyes. You're crazy as a bedbug. You're crazier than me."

I start to get mad again. I say, "Look, don't fuck with me. I just want to know where he is."

Brice says, "I don't know where he is. But I would like to fuck with you. Tender-like, if that's what you want. You can kiss away these tears."

I'm not sure if he's being serious or sarcastic. Both, I guess. But I say, "I don't think that would be a good idea."

He says, "Then get the hell out of here. If you don't want to fuck, then what's the point in talking? I'm wasting my time on you."

I'm not offended. The guy's drunk, he's hurting. Basically this naive kid who got in way over his head.

On the way to the door my heart kind of stops when I notice this leash and collar and an empty stainless steel bowl.

I say, "You've got a dog?"

He says, "Used to. He died a while back."

I say, "I'm sorry. I know how that is. I lost one too. A while back."

I look at him and I can tell he doesn't have a clue. I decide to leave him in the dark. I'm walking down the driveway when he calls to me from the trailer door: "I'm warning you. You do anything to him before he comes back to me, I'm gonna come after *you*."

So. I'm back on PCH now, heading south, back to town. A

good stretch of narrative road. Not too many stoplights or arbitrary text breaks. It's a beautiful day. Hot. Coming up on Zuma again. Tanned youth. Missed the beach traffic, that was good. It's about noon. Highway's clogged going the other way.

Lifeguard. There's something I could've worked into *Testosterone*. A *Lifeguard* variation. A positive, utopian fantasy, the film's dynamic homoeroticized. Not that it wasn't already, imagistically. Who could forget Sam Elliott's hairy dad chest in perpetual close proximity to Parker Stevenson's smooth boyish one. Hey, I know. I'm reading in. But that could've worked. In *Testosterone*, I mean. I'd be Sam. With my faithful, young, smooth, brown-skinned fellow lifeguard/slave Andy Garcia. Except actually Andy Garcia has a hairy chest and I don't. Oh well, that's the thing about drawing and computer art, as opposed to old-fashioned film. You can shuffle around all sorts of attributes.

Anyway, I'm trying to digest this. What just happened with Brice. Mostly this new information. I mean, the bondage stuff. It doesn't surprise me. Not at all. Not now. In fact, I had this crazy theory at one point that after what happened with me, Pablo probably kissed off "romantic" sex forever, and went straight into S/M. That if I really wanted to find him, I should start hitting the leather bars. And the thing is, most of my hunches about Pablo, my worst gut suspicions, have turned out to be true.

Like the tearoom thing. I mean, it's funny. Pablo didn't present himself as some sort of virgin exactly, who could? In fact, the first night, he made some remark about being surprised he'd tested negative since "I'm such a whore." Which at the time seemed almost charming. Or something. Or I just didn't care. I guess that was it. Knowing he was negative, I didn't care what he'd done: It suddenly didn't matter. Who was I to judge anyone, anyway?

But later he did create this impression of serial monogamy. Of having an aversion to scenes of mass sleaze. Like he told me he'd gone to that place, the Saint, in New York in his student days. Some vile disco/bathhouse that old New York sleaze queens are still wistful about, the three or four still alive anyway. But he made a point of saying, "Of course, I just danced. I didn't go upstairs." Right. I'll bet he had a dime in his purse too and was home by eleven. But at the time I believed him. Or did I?

One night we were going to get together and he called and canceled. Said he had to work on his paper. Fine. I went to a movie with Charlie. But afterward, I guiltily drove by the beach, the cruising beach where we'd met, to see if Pablo's car was there. I had no reason to be suspicious. That's why I felt guilty. I felt I was getting obsessed, getting paranoid. Well, his car wasn't there, but other cars were. And there were guys going into the tearoom. And I thought: What would I do if his car *was* there, if I walked into the tearoom and caught him? Then I thought: Oh, man, you're flipping out. You have a sick mind. He's not into that. Try and be a little trusting. If anyone's not into tearooms, it's Pablo.

Then, about two months after Pablo disappeared, I ran into Mark Spivey on the Venice boardwalk. This is a major scene, by the way. This was the true turning point.

I didn't really know Mark that well. I know him better now. That's where I'm headed, incidentally. Right now. I'm going to talk to Mark to see if he's heard anything.

James Robert Baker

So I knew Mark slightly. He'd been in Venice a long time, we had mutual friends. I'd been to a few of his shows. I like his work. And I'd realized that he was the "Mark" Pablo had gone with. The Mark who'd become "obsessed" with him, according to Pablo. The first time I put that together and said, "Oh, right. I know Mark," Pablo looked shaken. I know why now. He didn't want Mark and me comparing notes. He didn't want me talking to a previous victim. But at the time I thought he was just embarrassed, so I made a point of emphasizing that I didn't know Mark that well.

So Mark stops me on the boardwalk, and at first it's just small talk. Then he says, "You know, I almost called you a while back. I heard you were going with Pablo Ortega."

I say, "Yeah, I was. But we broke up."

And Mark says, "Well, you know, I actually tracked down your number, but then I hesitated. I wasn't sure if I should interfere. If I should warn you or not."

I say, "Warn me about what?"

He says, "Well, Pablo is an emotional serial killer. He sets guys up, and as soon as they let their guard down, he eviscerates them." He says, "Are you OK?"

I say, "Yeah, I'm fine. We just broke up. It just didn't work out. It wasn't that messy, though."

Mark says, "Well, you're lucky. You're very lucky. He ax-murdered me. I mean, it was crazy. Really like a serial killer. We went together for about three months. We were close, it was intense, that's the way I am. Together every night. We fucked every night. And I guess I don't have to tell you what the sex was like. Then one night he turned on me, in this totally unprovoked psycho way. Like a different personality or something. I'll never forget the look in his eyes. Like an animal honing in for the kill. That's what he did. Verbally. I can't even tell you what he said, it's too vile. Because I'd told him things, personal things, painful things from childhood. Things you should really only tell a therapist, I guess. But I trusted him. He'd told me similar things about himself. Assuming any of it, or anything he ever said, was true. But he was out to kill me that night, verbally. If words can kill, and I think they can. He said things about my body. Look, I know I'm a few pounds overweight. But it wasn't just that. He expressed such loathing, such revulsion and disgust. Which didn't equate with the way we'd had sex. I know I turned him on. Why would he fake it? He had no motive. So it didn't equate."

Mark went on in this calm tone of voice, which was kind of deceptive. I mean, later I wished I'd stopped him. I wished I'd said: Mark, I don't want to hear this, I can't handle this. But at the time I didn't realize what he was doing. That he was turning me into the instrument of his revenge. Of course, I couldn't react honestly, since I was already lying. Trying to act like nothing was wrong, like Pablo and I had had this mature, mutually agreed-upon breakup. So I just stood there listening. And another thing: Mark's not a queen. He has this easy-going blond boyish thing, kind of David Lynch crossed with Eric Fischl. So he didn't seem like some obviously bitter jilted queen launching a bitch attack. Even though I tried to tell myself later that's what had been going on.

He said, he kind of tossed off, "Of course, at first he stopped the tearooms."

And I thought: The what? The fucking what?

"At first," Mark said, "he was counting the days. He got up

to twenty-three days, then he stopped mentioning it. So that's when I knew he was doing it again."

I said, "You think he was into tearooms?"

Mark said, "Look, he knew it was a problem for him. I'll give him credit for that. That's why he went to SCA [Sexual Compulsives Anonymous]. Look, I was in no position to judge him. God knows, I'm probably a sex addict myself—if I wanted to give myself that label. I mean, I have no doubt that's where I picked up you-know-what."

Well, by this point I'm shitting. I'm shitting right there on the boardwalk. He's telling me that Pablo is a tearoom queen. He's telling me that probably while I thought we were being monogamous Pablo was coming in with some other guy's spit on his crank, with God knows what in his mouth when I kissed him. If that's not fucked enough, Mark's also telling me he's got HIV, and I know beyond any doubt that Pablo must have at the very least chowed down innumerable times on Mark's crank. So of course I'm even wondering if Pablo was lying about his status. Or, charitably, if he might have snagged the virus from Mark, but it just hadn't shown up on the test yet. So I'm shitting. I'm standing there imploding.

Mark says at one point about Pablo's tearoom behavior, "He *claimed* he was mostly a voyeur." Of course, that makes me feel much better. As long as he was *mostly* a voyeur. Just sniffing around the urinals, eyeing other men's peters. Or taking in the view through the peepholes. Only very rarely actually wrapping his lips around a stranger's smegma-coated prod.

Mark tells me Pablo liked the action at UCLA. Mark had gone to art school there and one day he stopped by the campus with Pablo. "Before I could introduce him to several old friends, they were all going, 'Oh, yes. We know *Pablo.*' With knowing leers. Like every tearoom queen on campus has fooled around with Pablo. Imagine how I felt. I hate to admit this, but I thought we were in love."

I was very understanding. But stated again that it hadn't really been that bad for me. That I'd just realized at a certain point that Pablo and I had nothing in common except the sex, which was admittedly pretty good but obviously not enough to sustain a relationship. So it seemed best if we went our separate ways. I don't know if Mark really bought this or not.

As soon as I got to my car, I blew. Pounding the steering wheel, the whole bit. Look, I'm a hothead. I have a temper, that's no secret. But this time I got mad—and *stayed mad.* And this was something I'd never experienced before. This *sustained* level of rage. This thing of wanting to kill someone. Not just for a few minutes, but over a period of days and weeks. Because that's what I wanted to do. I lived on rage through the month of September, till it started to make me physically sick.

So that was the turning point, talking to Mark. Which in one way was good. At least I could stop blaming myself, scouring my brain to figure out what I'd done to make Pablo mad at me, to drive him away. But the downside was this. I didn't feel better knowing he'd done it before. I felt like a woman who'd gone out with Ted Bundy and thought he was a super guy. I felt like a chump. I hadn't done anything. It wasn't my fault. But the question remained: Why had he picked me? Was I putting out something I didn't know about? Was there a sign stuck on my back that said "Easy Prey"?

So that was the turning point. Up to then I'd been rational.

I'd been confused, I'd been hurt, I'd been a lot of things, but not homicidal. I'd been where Brice is now, although I hate to admit it. But I had the same fantasies. That Pablo would miss me, that he'd call or just show up. I'd open the door, and he'd have tears in his eyes. "Dean, I'm so sorry. I just got scared, that's all." That kind of shit. I'd started seeing *Twin Peaks* Bob. I'd been trying to figure out what I'd done wrong.

Now, thanks to Mark, I just felt like a chump, the chump of the century, which is something I'm not into. Maybe some people get off on feeling like a chump, but I'm not one of them. I mean, part of it was the cheating, the idea that he'd been having these tearoom trysts behind my back. Because even though he was on leave, he'd still go out to Cal Tech to do research, where he could take a "study break." And, of course, there were places much closer. I knew some of them. Look, I can't say I've never had tearoom sex, that I've never been sucked off through a glory hole. But I was never a total fiend about it, and I haven't gone to tearooms for a really long time, not since AIDS. And it was never my arena of choice, so to speak.

But the point is this: We were supposed to be monogamous. I mean, we'd discussed it, we had a formal agreement. Which is supposed to mean something, I think, even to two gay men. Right? I mean, I hate to bring up anything as old-fashioned as ethics or morals or fidelity in relation to two gay men, but I'll risk it. Especially now. I mean it's not just a question of a slight, charming peccadillo, we're talking about life and death. So I'm thinking that Pablo's probably killed me. That I probably got AIDS because my goddamn boyfriend was a secret fucking sleazy little scumbag beaner tearoom queen. Except, of course, I don't know for certain that I have it, since at this point I haven't taken the test yet. So I think about taking it and it pisses me off that I waited till now, since if I come up positive now, there'll be no way to know for certain that I got it from Pablo. Because if I could tell for certain that he gave it to me, I'd have nothing to lose, so I'd definitely kill him.

Of course, I'm ultimately still hoping that he's really negative despite whatever sleazy shit he's done. But I feel like my whole life is riding on whether he's in fact "mostly a voyeur" on his sojourns through the Ortonian netherworld of overflowing toilets and grim men with boners. So I still want to kill him.

I talk to *Twin Peaks* Bob about this. Which is strange, since he's straight. I mean, the whole thing, talking to him about what happened with Pablo, which is the whole reason I went to him in the first place. Jack had gone to see him once and said he was cool, not homophobic. Which I guess was true. He had other gay patients. I saw a slim young queen in his waiting room once. But you know how it is with straight people. No matter how open-minded they are, you have a feeling that at a certain point they're going to think: My God, if I have to hear any more of this *fag shit* I'm going to start screaming. Screaming in a masculine way, of course. A John Wayne scream. Bob did admit once that back in the sixties he'd had the "arrogance" to think he could cure homosexuals. Glad you got over that arrogance, Bob. Or learned how much more money you could make by listening to fags talk about their fucked-up relationships and pretending you think all that sick shit is normal. I mean, you always have this feeling he's going to say to his girlfriend, "Man, this one fruit patient I've got now..."

So why I did keep going to this guy? I don't know, except he wasn't all bad, despite the way I just trashed him. He made some interesting connections between Pablo and my father. ACA [Adult Children of Alcoholics] stuff, I guess, but I won't get into all that now. You know the line. Withholding father. So you keep seeking Dad's approval from similar withholding men. That's it right there, basically. He could've said that the first session and saved me hundreds of dollars.

Except it wasn't cheap insight I was after. I needed to blow off steam. And Bob was good for that. I mean, I could talk about wanting to kill Pablo and he wouldn't get all weird and antsy the way some prissy gay shrink might. At least that's how I figured it. Not that all gay shrinks are prissy. But here's the problem with Bob. I think I might have gotten into trying to prove something. Like: OK, I may be gay, but I'm as violent as any straight guy. Something like that. *I ain't no nelly-belle, I wanna kill mah ex-boyfriend!* Not that I didn't have those feelings all on my own, before I saw Bob. And I'm not sure how much he really cooled me out. Not that he said, "Do it" or anything. He usually tried to make light of it or treat it as a joke. Like we'd got to the point where we could joke about it, humor as a sign of returning mental health. So I joked about it. But still wanted to do it.

That was the worst period, though. That whole period last fall. Because at that point all I knew about was Pablo's tearoom stuff, his sex addict stuff, the presumed infidelity, and that he'd eviscerated others before me. I knew there were others, even before Mark. Mark had mentioned that. But I didn't know any more yet. I didn't want to know. I knew why I was mad, it seemed understandable, but I was still at the point where I wanted to put it behind me. I didn't want this fucked-up affair to rule me for the rest of my life. Or make me scared to ever trust anyone again. I mean, I've seen that happen. Where people just give up. Jay is like that. I don't know the details. But someone broke his heart about, Jesus, ten years ago. And look at him now. I mean, I like Jay, which is the point. That's why I think it's a shame. He got fat, turned himself into this celibate slug who only lives in his mind, through his art. It's sad. He wasn't bad-looking in the old days. But he's given up. He's two years younger than me, so I don't think age is a factor. Unless he has different standards or values than me. I mean, he threw in the towel, he surrendered to male spinsterhood, at the ripe old peaked-out age of twenty-six.

So I was trying to "process" all this. I hate that word, that's Charlie's word, and I'm not even sure if I believe in the whole concept of "processing" experiences. I think it may turn you into a bar of Velveeta. What I mean is I see people processing the same things again and again for years, for decades. So I wonder if that happened to me. Was I getting out of my anger at Pablo by talking about it? Or getting deeper into it? Was it becoming my new identity? The one who is angry at Pablo. The one who wants to kill Pablo. Pablo Killer, *qu'est-ce que c'est*? It's Talking Heads weekend. But I'm joking now. I'm trying to be witty and I'm not even sure why. I'm passing the Malibu Colony now.

So where was I? Oh, right, it's last fall and I'm trying to get over Pablo. Release my rage. So I can move on. So the last thing I need is any new information or evidence. So I really don't want to see Mark again. This is the period where I was blaming Mark. Feeling set up to do his dirty work or something. Except I have to say this. These homicidal feelings I had, this wanting to kill Pablo, were just that: feelings. I mean, I wanted to, I fantasized. Not elaborately, not cold-bloodedly. But I'd think if I saw him I'd do this or that. Shove his face through a window, cut his jugular vein on the glass. Bash his head against the floor again and again till his skull cracked like Nicolas Cage did to that guy in *Wild at Heart*. Things like that. Big cathartic rage situations, like crimes of passion. But I wasn't looking for him at this point. I wasn't getting a weapon.

But here's why that was such a bad period. Because the more I stayed mad, the longer it went on, the more it seemed like there was something wrong with me. So in spite of what he'd done, I began to think: I should be over this by now. It's been five, then six months. I should be over this. Any sane, normal person would be over this by now. Movie stars get divorced and remarry six weeks later. What's *wrong* with me? Why I am still thinking about this piece-of-shit scumbag beaner?

This was before I fully realized just how he'd set me up. I was naive about certain things, I bought into certain cultural myths, especially that *Fatal Attraction* version of obsession. I mean, I've been on the receiving end of that. You know, the thing that happened with Ray, years ago. Back then I thought of *Play Misty for Me*. I was Clint and he was Jessica. You know that story. It got pretty crazy, like the night he lay down in front of my car. But it blew over. We're friendly now.

But I didn't really identify with the other side of that equation. I mean, I had problems with that movie, with *Fatal*

Attraction, on a metaphoric level. Seeing Glenn Close as libido or something, in opposition to the insipid nuclear family. I mean, it's a very reactionary film, the same way fifties sci-fi and horror films were. The big thing about the threatened family.

But in terms of the main dynamic, I identified with Michael Douglas. Thinking of Ray, no doubt, at that point. Thinking how Ray had been like what's-her-name, Alex. Although Ray never boiled my bunny. Or poured acid on my car, he just lay down in front of it. But the point is this: I've had some strange relationships, and they haven't all ended on polite, cordial notes. But I don't have some big history of getting all obsessed with people in a big psycho way, like Glenn Close. So when *Twin Peaks* Bob mentioned that film, when he made that allusion, it kind of stopped me in my tracks. Because of course I realized that's what was going on. Somehow, when I wasn't looking, I'd become Glenn Close.

Which, to be blunt, I found very mortifying, which is not something I'm into. I'm sure some people are, in a city the size of Los Angeles. They probably run ads: "Into heavy mortification." But I would never run that ad, because that's not me. So I was glad I was keeping my mouth shut. With my friends, I mean. Except Charlie. He was the one person, besides *Twin Peaks* Bob, I really talked to. But even with Charlie I put up a certain front. He was glad I was seeing a therapist, he'd strongly recommended it, so I acted like I was getting all better.

But I felt like Glenn Close. Which was scary and awful. And it didn't really help much, it didn't give me much relief, when I began to see that was what Pablo wanted. He'd positioned

James Robert Baker

me to feel like Glenn Close. He *wanted* me to feel like some obsessed psycho. That was the game he'd been playing all along. My big mistake was this: I didn't see it as a game. I wasn't playing a game. I was trying to be honest and open.

But I thought about all this—

TAPE 2

OK, this is tape two. Where was I? Oh, right. So I thought about this whole *Fatal Attraction* thing. I thought about it all in an entirely new way, and I began to see certain things. For starters, I saw how wrong the analogy was for my situation, how bad it was, how to glibly suggest that I was Glenn Close, as *Twin Peaks* Bob had, was this totally wrongheaded smear. Because for starters Pablo is not Michael Douglas. He didn't have some Anne Archer somewhere. It wasn't like we'd had a brief sex affair, with a dinner scene at my apartment where he made a big point of saying he wasn't ever going to leave his little wifey-poo. Since of course he didn't fucking have one. What he *did* do was everything he possibly could to convince me that he was in love with me—short of actually using that word. But I mean, we were boyfriends; we used that word. And we had this monogamous commitment. We had this *relationship*, a word I don't like, but that's what it was. We hadn't talked about living together, which was a choice on my part, not to get into that yet. I mean, I know some people meet and move in together two weeks later. But I was cautious, I guess. Or I had this sense that because it was so intense I wanted to wait and see if we could take it to the next, lower key level. Or maybe I just sensed certain things about him, the same way I had these cheating suspicions. I don't think you can do the things Pablo has done without something foul rubbing off. It's just not possible. You can wash your hands and get rid of the smell, the literal stench, but something intangible has to remain.

But the main thing I saw from deconstructing *Fatal Attraction* was what was in it for the Michael Douglas figure. I mean, the ego trip. I saw it by reflecting on how I'd felt when I was the object of Ray's obsession. I remember talking about that once at dinner with Charlie and some other guy, while it was going on, how I was freaked out that Ray might do something violent. This was at the point where he was still calling me all the time, trying to have a reconciliation. And this other guy said something like, "Boy, you must be *hot sex* to have a guy that flipped out over you." Hot sex, good in bed, a hot fuck, something like that. And of course I enjoyed the remark. That's my point. It's very flattering to have someone obsessed with you. It's a very good advertisement. It's a sympathetic role. You can act distraught and also seem sane, unlike the other person. But tacitly you're also saying: I'm just too much. People can't get enough of me. When they can't have me, they just go insane.

Which of course fit in neatly with Pablo's sex-god riff. So that's when I saw how he'd positioned me. And why he'd ended it the way he had. I think he knew it would fuck with my head worse than anything if he just walked out, disappeared, without any explanation. It almost seems too obvious, too heavy-handed, but I did tell him about my father. How my father essentially did the same thing to my mother and me. He didn't go out for cigarettes. He just didn't come home from work one night. He drove to Las Vegas with his secretary. But it was similar. I mean, my mom was in shock. She was like June Cleaver. With Ward suddenly calling from Las Vegas, saying, "It's over." And I was twelve and, you know, had never got along with my father. So I also thought it was something I'd done.

I don't know if Pablo did this consciously, or if he just had an instinct for honing in on people's pain. It's not an important question. The point is, he did it. I mean, when Mark first told me what Pablo had done to *him*, I thought I was lucky. That at least Pablo didn't attack me verbally. I thought maybe it was better that he just disappeared. Then I began to see how he did it that way deliberately so there wouldn't be closure. So I'd have to go on thinking about him. He wanted that. He likes the idea of lots of guys out there with broken hearts, if that's what you want to call it. It feeds his ego. That's one thing I've learned from this that's scary. People will do anything to feed their egos, anything at all. So you damn well better watch out.

❉ ❉ ❉

Passing Santa Monica Canyon now. Always think of Christopher Isherwood, *A Single Man*. That's a good book, a classic. There's the Friendship. That's been there a long time. Isherwood used it in his novel...shit, thirty years ago. Called it something else though. The Shipwreck or something. It's closed up now. The place next door fell into it during the quake. Bet it reopens, though. It's OK, except when they play Cher on the jukebox. "If I Could Turn Back Time." Not without another butt-lift, darlin'. Is that what that tattoo's all about? To hide the butt-lift scars?

So everybody's going to the Rooster Fish now. That's the only other gay bar on this side of town. Excluding the lesbian dives in Culver City or wherever they are. Maybe I should find out. If I became a dyke, that would solve all my problems. It's tempting.

But the Rooster Fish is OK. They've got a good jukebox. Morrissey, New Order, early Bryan Ferry. That's where I met Frank last spring. The yoga instructor. But I'm getting ahead of myself.

Here's what happened. I stopped seeing *Twin Peaks* Bob and took the AIDS test.

The way it ended with Bob was very undramatic. I just got sick of repeating myself. I reached this point of burnout talking about Pablo. And he was into short-term therapy, as opposed to stringing you along for years. So we hugged, and he crawled back across the sofa, and that was it.

I still don't know why I took the AIDS test. I swore I'd never take it. You know where I was at. I didn't want to know. I didn't want to have to live with that knowledge, if it went the wrong way. But I guess I just got tired of mind-fucking myself. Probably have it, probably don't. Probably do, probably don't. That went on for ten fucking years! So I said, fuck it, let's find out, and went to this clinic. Had to wait two days. I don't want to be dramatic, but I was clutching the ceiling. My heart didn't stop pounding for two solid days. It was the worst thing I've ever had to do. By far, the worst.

Because I'm not one of these positive-thinking people. Like it's not necessarily a death sentence. You just go on The Cocktail and exercise, watch your diet, keep an upbeat attitude, and everything will be fine. I don't believe that. I don't want to be downbeat, but I just don't buy it. I've seen way too many people croak.

And here's the thing. It wasn't just me who was going to die if it had gone the other way. I'd made this decision. That if I had it, I was going to track Pablo down and kill him. Of course, I'd have no way of knowing if he gave it me, or if I'd had it before we met, but that wasn't even important. I'd have nothing to lose, and I felt I'd be doing other people a favor. I'd be saving future victims, like Brice. Not that my motives were all noble. I'm not trying to pretend that. Eighty percent of it was just plain revenge. Maybe that's why I also anticipated turning the gun on myself once I killed him. Eating the gun. So I wouldn't have to stand trial, die of AIDS a few years later in prison. I was going to use a gun. I looked up the gun shops in the yellow pages, circled one in Culver City.

So it was very existential, those two days of waiting. I saw my life going one way or the other. That was the upside. I realized viscerally that I wanted to live. That my true and ultimate dream was to live a long life where I could be creative and have positive friendships and loving relationships, to sing in the sunshine and all that. This other road, this film noir alternative, was a bad second choice. Going out in a big, cathartic

Taxi Driver bloodbath was preferable to a long, slow, agonizing AIDS death, but it was not what I really wanted. It was not my dark secret dream. So it was strange. It's hard to explain, but during those two days I realized that in some very deep basic way I was not a bad person. I might be fucked up in various ways, damaged, etcetera, but who isn't? But at base I was not an evil person. My ultimate dream was creation, not destruction. So I was really hoping for the best.

I kind of knew it was negative before I drove in to get the results in person. If it had gone the other way, it would've taken more time, to run the Western Blot test or something. So when I called and they said they had the results, I was pretty sure I was OK. Unless it was a bad joke or something. So I didn't really celebrate or anything till I heard the words, "Your test was negative."

Even then I didn't react the way I'd thought I might. I didn't start sobbing or anything. I was glad, needless to say, but also in a strange kind of shock.

But that was the turning point for the better. As the days went by I began to feel that I had a kind of second chance. It was seven months at this point since I'd had sex with Pablo, so I was reasonably sure I hadn't gotten it from him. I began to think that maybe he really was negative. Maybe he and Mark did have safe sex—or saf*er* sex or whatever. Suddenly the whole thing seemed like history, truly behind me. One thing about testing negative, you can close a lot of files. Old boyfriends, different encounters. Did I get it there? Did I give it to them? You can stamp all those cases closed. And for a while that's what I did with the file on Pablo Ortega.

All through the period after the breakup I'd been working

on *Foto-Novella*. At times I seemed to be working by rote, since I had the whole thing so thoroughly planned out. But I think in some ways it saved me. If I hadn't been working, God knows what my mind would've done, considering what it did anyway. But then I finished *Foto-Novella* and I knew it was good, and then I sold the film rights almost immediately, so I didn't have to worry about money for a while. And the reviews were almost all good, so I was glad I'd kept at it, even through the period where I lost my sense of humor, where I had no idea why I'd ever thought any of it was funny or satiric. But I trusted that at one point, before Pablo, I'd known what I was doing. And the reviews were vindicating that way.

Then I made what may have been a big mistake. I took a break and went to Mexico with Charlie and thought about what I wanted to do next. I had all these different ideas, including the one I'd planned to do next, the TV child star idea. I think I told you about that. It's been developing for almost six years, and on paper it's always a good idea. And big enough culturally to have wide appeal. But something always stops me from sitting down and doing it. It's always the next thing I'm going to do, but something else, more compelling, always comes up instead.

This time it was *Testosterone*. I don't know where the initial idea came from, I can't really trace it back. But I think it had something to do with Manuel Puig and Andy Garcia. With Rita Hayworth and Pablo's mother. Since that's what she was at one time, an actress. The Rita Hayworth of Mexico, according to Pablo. Which seems like a strange, twisted thing to be. Since Rita Hayworth was herself Mexican but tried to hide it and pass for Anglo. So I thought of that Manuel Puig novel

[*Betrayed by Rita Hayworth*], and then I thought of Andy Garcia in *Internal Affairs*. This whole macho competition routine teetering on the edge of homoeroticism. So that's how it started, this idea of a fabulist graphic novel. And I thought at this point the dust had settled enough for me to use what had happened, transmute it. I always knew it could be dangerous. That I could stir myself up again. I knew I'd have to, if it was going to be any good. But I felt I could handle it. I believed that if my heart was pure I'd be protected. I believed in the alchemy of art.

So I began *Testosterone* as an experiment. I didn't know if it would work or not. It was a kind of radical next step, so I wasn't sure if it would pan out. I mean, you know how I feel about narrative. But this was something else. This was not a pastiche. Unless you think that dreams are just pastiches. Which I guess some critic could say. I mean, I have chase dreams, thriller dreams, cheap-suspense dreams that are completely cinematic. Genre dreams. So I was incorporating all these different elements. But I didn't know where it was going from one day to the next. I made a point of not knowing. It wasn't preplanned. It was almost like automatic drawing. I did it in a kind of trance state.

So the first time I took a break and really looked at what I'd done I was very excited. When I looked at it critically. I felt as if I'd accessed a new part of my brain. Which was very exciting. I even felt it had all been worth it, what I'd gone through with Pablo, if it led to this. That's how much I believe in art. Everything else on a certain level is just there to serve it. Which may not be too healthy, but I don't give a shit.

So I was drawing Pablo essentially. Calling him Paco. And

this thing began to happen, which maybe you've experienced, since your writing is so autobiographical. But I hadn't, since I was used to "inventing" in a certain way. I mean, I drew on real people for *Foto-Novella*, but in a much larger, less personal way. But here, with *Testosterone*, I was working with someone I'd been involved with, had all these strong feelings about, so I could really see this process of transmutation taking place. The "real" Pablo becoming less and less important. Superseded by the fictional Pablo, or Paco. Until it suddenly occurred to me one day: My God, I've contained, I've embalmed, I've *aestheticized* another human being.

Not that I felt this was a bad thing. On the contrary, I felt that it was something that had to be done. It's worth pointing out that *Testosterone* is not vicious. It's not a big blistering attack. The permutations of the characters, Paco and Skip, are complex and shifting. It's not like one's good and one's bad. It's an ongoing battle, approach and avoidance, hide and seek. They both have flawed characters. They both have good intentions. So it's not like I was out to do some hatchet job.

But at a certain point I began to have a funny feeling, which I now think was guilt that I was disposing of a real person so easily. But at the time I saw it as the birth of disinterested compassion.

This happened when I came to the subterranean tearoom sequence. That's what I called it, since that was the setting. In fact, it came from some nightmares I'd had in the eighties. About being in some sort of weird, labyrinthine men's room. A massive 1930s marble-walled facility, with dozens of stalls, row after row, all filled with men having sex though glory holes and strange open panels between the partitions. In these nightmares, I'd be both drawn and repelled. A part of me wanting to join the action. But I'd always see someone with lesions, or in some way there'd be this sense of disease in the air. So I'd be afraid to join in, and I'd be angry that I couldn't.

But when it came time to draw this, and work Pablo into it, I suddenly became uncertain about what I wanted to say. I stopped to think about it, instead of working from my subconscious. Then I decided I didn't want to just trash him. I didn't just want to make him look sleazy. I wanted to imbue the sequence with some sort of compassion. That's where that word came in. But I wasn't sure how to do it. Or how I felt about this whole subject of anonymous sex. So I decided to do some research. At least that's what I told myself when I went to SCA.

But right now I'm in Venice. Turning onto Speedway. It's hot. It's a fucking zoo down here today. Some nice-looking guys, though. There's a pack.

OK, I'm coming to Breeze now. What are you looking at? Some airhead's staring at me, thinks I'm talking to myself. Fuck you, honey. Mind your own business. I should have a car phone or something.

So here's Breeze. Fuck it, I'm parking in the red zone. I'll be back in a while.

✳   ✳   ✳

Hi. Well, Mark's not home, and I'm a little worried. It's probably nothing, but there's a bunch of mail on his floor. I looked in through the slot. I mean, he's probably up north. Or maybe he went to New Mexico again. Then again, he might be in the hospital. That's my fear. It's really sad. Except what can you say that isn't inadequate at this point? Sad? I guess it doesn't really matter what you say at this point. Dietrich was right in *Touch of Evil* when she said: "What does it matter what you say about people?"

So anyway, I'm thinking. I'm trying to decide what's next. This is kind of a set-back. This is not unfolding smoothly. To be honest, I thought Mark would know where Pablo was. That's what I expected. So I'm kind of back to square one. Not that I'm giving up. Far from it. I still have this very special feeling about today.

But right now I'm going to get out of here. Before I get a ticket. As long as I'm in Venice, I might as well swing by the Love Street house. Which might take a while, at the rate we're going here. This is gridlock on the Speedway. I'm beginning to hate L.A. I used to say it was love/hate. But it's turning into hate/hate. There are too many people and they're all pissed off. The principle's the same as *Day of the Locust*. They come here looking for their dreams but instead find their nightmares. Only the volume has changed. It's like another half million blow into town each month. And the crime is worse. It's more vicious. Now you've got moms caught in gang crossfires, their babies shot out of their arms. Look, I grew up here. I remember when the gas and marijuana were cheap, when you could still experience freeway euphoria, when Southern California was a white boy's utopia. The days of fun, fun, fun. Before the killers of color shot you in the head and took your T-bird away.

White boy. That's a title. *White Boy*. It's also the name of John Singleton's cat. You know, [the African-American director of] *Boyz N the Hood*. I read that in a profile. He lives in Baldwin Hills with a cat named White Boy. Which reminds me of a news story. About a black guy who flipped out and stabbed a white guy in the neck. Because the white guy had given his dog a racial slur for a name. They didn't say what the name was on the news, like they didn't want to repeat it. Which, of course, only set off a big guessing game as to what the fuck it was. Here, Nigger. Roll over, Jungle Bunny. Fetch, Darkie. Good dog, Jigaboo. Down, Coon.

But White Boy? I saw an ad with that phrase a while back in the *L.A. Weekly*. "Hey, white boy, wanna play?" That's how it opened. It was from a GM Latino, thirty-two, HIV-. There was something sadistic about it, in the wording. I don't remember exactly how it went, but the subtext seemed to be: If you want some Latino guy to treat you like shit, call now. It jolted me, and I had a premonition. That it was Pablo, a year later, having gone more overt. I felt weird, but I called the number, just to see if it was him. It's wasn't, though. I got a recording, but it wasn't his voice. I thought about leaving a message anyway. "Suck my fat white cock, you scumbag beaner spic." But I've made an effort through all this not to get racist. And I haven't. I really don't think I have. Not that I'll be cowed into the opposite, into saying that all Latinos are wonderful. Just because it's the PC thing to say. I look at people as individuals, to quote Abraham Lincoln. Or was it Pinkie Lee? I've had good experiences with Latino guys. Like Steven, ten years ago, and Raul. That's why I know I'm not racist. Which doesn't mean I'm going to endorse every aspect of Latino culture as intrinsically wondrous. I have serious problems, for example, with Catholicism. I think they're murderers; all the churches should be dynamited. ACT UP didn't go far enough at St. Patrick's. Not far enough at all. They should've gone in with AK-47s, spread some serious lead. It's a religion of pain and agony, a bunch of fussy decorations and crackpot ritual built on a corpse heap. I think the pope should be dismembered, Serbian chainsaw-style, one joint at a time. It's also Chicken Hawk Central. Our Lady of the Pedophile. But I'm getting off the track. I'll come back to all this later. This Latino stuff especially. But I wonder if the *Weekly* would let me place an ad that said: "Hey, brown boy, wanna play?" I don't think so, knowing them.

I don't believe this. I'm still on the fucking Speedway. This is absurd. It's a good thing I'm not in a hurry. I mean, you don't have to rush to keep an appointment with fate.

So SCA. Yeah, I want to mention that. I went to SCA, which was edifying. A big meeting in some church, some raunchy church, in West Hollywood. At Fountain and Fairfax. So of course walking in I was somewhat apprehensive. I mean, my heart was pounding. On the chance that Pablo would be there. I really don't know what I would've done. Except that's not completely true. If I'm honest anyway, I know what I *wanted*. It might not have happened. Probably, if he'd been there, he would've made a quick exit as soon as he saw me. A quick, angry exit. But what I wanted was this. I didn't want to kill him anymore. I wanted us to make up. That's the truth of it. Which is crazy, I know. It had been seven, eight months at this point, and I'd spent half that time wanting to kill him. But so what? People have extreme emotions. Love and hate are very close. I'm just being honest. I'm not saying it's sane or anything. But in the back of my mind that was my ultimate fantasy. That I'd run into him there, and we'd talk and one thing would lead to another. I still had this sense that he couldn't reject me to my face. This goes back to the sexual dynamic. Seeing me face to face I knew he'd want me again, the same way I still wanted him. In fact, enough time had passed that he might be kicking himself for having gotten so scared. This was partially egotism, no doubt. But I knew we'd had something sexually that you don't find every day. Maybe he saw that now.

But he wasn't there.

It was interesting though. An eclectic crowd. I don't know what I expected. Maybe not so many really young guys, for one thing. By really young, I mean in their early twenties. I guess I had this sense there'd be more guys my age, late thirties/early forties, who were trying to overcome old patterns from the pre-AIDS years. Of course, that applies to Pablo, despite our age difference. I still think of him as thirty, but he's really thirty-two now.

So people "shared" and all that, like an AA meeting, and it became apparent that most of them were recovering tearoom queens. Some of the stories were pretty extreme. In terms of numbers. Like one young college guy, nice-looking guy. I mean, he could've snagged a boyfriend just on that level. But he was saying he'd just had sex with twenty guys that afternoon at UCLA. Hard not to see that as compulsive.

Of course, I heard things that I related to. I'll readily admit that I've used sex as a drug at times in my life. But I see it like this. I was able to stop on my own. The same way there was a time I was kind of into food. My first year in college. Then

I changed my eating habits and permanently lost weight. Without going to Overeaters Anonymous. Like maybe I stopped it while I still had some control. That's the way I see this sex thing. I've never gone out and had sex with twenty people. Maybe I backed off before it came to that.

So I had mixed feelings about this whole trip. On the one hand, I was all for it. I know how destructive anonymous sex can be, emotionally destructive. And with AIDS, it's a whole other thing. So I felt: Good, at least these guys are dealing with it, they see it as a problem, and they're trying to change.

The part I didn't like was the censorship. That's how I thought of it. They asked people not to use inflammatory language. No, *sensational* language, that was it. In other words, not to say, "This guy shoved his big fat cock through the glory hole and shot come all over my face this afternoon." Things that would set people off. Or make them want to act out. I understood, but I have a different relationship to language, I guess. To me, words, especially on a certain level of verbal imagery, have an almost discrete reality. I don't feel they're going to *make me* go out and do things. Any more than pornography *made* Ted Bundy kill. So there seemed to be some blame shifting involved.

Also, I guess, I come from a generation that fought so hard for the right of free expression that any attempt anywhere to reprudify the language really sets me off. So that bothered me. The way people had to watch what they said, which led to a kind of coy, elliptical way of speaking. Like a fuck film recut to get a PG-13.

But in other ways I found the meetings interesting. I went to several more over the next few weeks. It had a strangely humanizing effect. To see different guys I found very attractive. Guys I might have had sex with, say, at the beach. Without thinking of how they felt at the time. That they might be suicidal, at the end of a four-day sex binge. So it made me aware in a strange way of the intrinsic callousness of objectifying people. Even when it's consensual.

There was also a lot of childhood-abuse talk. A lot of literal incest, as opposed to emotional incest and these other more nebulous terms. So naturally I wondered about Pablo. Because he'd never talked much about his father. He'd been a journalist in Chile, that was about all I knew. His parents got divorced when Pablo was nine, in 1972. That's when his mother brought him to L.A. His father was dead. Pablo never said so, but somehow I got the idea his father had been a *left-wing* journalist, who was killed after the '73 coup. Later, I wished I'd pressed him more about his father, since that's such an important dynamic. But Pablo was good at closing certain subjects off, so you'd feel like you were prying if you asked.

So most of the guys were tearoom queens, or sex club queens, essentially into *normal* compulsive sex. The two extreme things I heard involved animals and shit, respectively. Some guy as a Midwestern boy did it with his dog. Don't ask me any more; I don't know. The other guy, who'd been into S/M, I guess, had once gone so far as to "taste" shit, although he hadn't actually eaten it. That, he feared, would be the inevitable next step.

What can I say? I know I'm vanilla, and I have a weak stomach when it comes to scat. I mean, when I heard this, I was looking around for the barf bag. I feel for the guy. He had AIDS, incidentally. But *shit*—I don't know, what can you say? I'm getting queasy right now, just thinking about it.

But here we are, at last. Love Street. Rialto really, but Pablo and I rented *The Doors* one night, and that was the best thing in it. The Venice "Love Street" house, which was actually over on the canals. But this place here, especially at night, has the same juicy, fruity, seething psychedelic carnival-light feeling. The kind of place where you'd like to take acid and fuck all night. Which is what we used to do here, except we didn't need the acid. But this is where he put me under his spell, figuratively if not in some other way.

I don't know who lives here now. Yuppies, I guess. A straight couple who think they're bohemian. I've seen the woman getting out of her Volvo.

I've driven by a few times before. Once when I was angry. But mostly later, during the time I've been describing, during the SCA period, when I was feeling compassionate, if that's what it was. I'm pulling over now. I guess I can park here for a minute. Jesus, it's getting hot. All this talking is making me thirsty.

So I'd drive by here sometimes and think about how it had been. I mean, about when it was good. When I'd come over. Except here's the strange thing. I never spent the night here. It wasn't convenient, since Pablo was using the guest room, which just had a single bed. He never really explained why he didn't use the main bedroom, which presumably had a double bed. I never saw that room. The door was always closed. Later, when I found out the owner had actually died of AIDS, I thought that might have been the reason. It would've been too spooky to use the guy's bed, which was possibly his deathbed. I don't know all the details. Except I do know this. The guy was an old friend of Pablo's, one of his oldest friends, from high school in Granada Hills. So they were just friends, not boyfriends, which I thought at one point. But it was impractical to sleep on a single bed, so I'd always go home afterwards when we had sex here. Which was strange in a way. But then he'd come up to my place and stay over, so it seemed OK.

One thing about Pablo, his skin was really amazing. So smooth and warm. Sometimes that was the best part, when I first put my arms around him. When we'd get into bed. The shock of first contact. The first kiss. That could be the best part. I got so comfortable with him, but it never got boring. It just got better. But here's the crazy part. I can still start to get turned on just thinking about him, about what it was like. Even now. Which you don't understand yet, why that's so insane. But you will. There's a lot I haven't gotten into yet.

But trust me for now when I tell you it's insane to still have these feelings for Pablo Ortega. It is morally appalling, and some would judge me harshly. Priests would, I know. As if I were *choosing* to be aroused. But I understand it. It's Pavlovian. Pablo conditioned me. So I don't blame myself. I'm like an ex-addict, a former speed freak. I'll never forget what the rush was like, and sometimes I'll still long for it. But it's the drug I long for, or the high. Not the person who got me addicted.

They've painted this house. They've fixed it up. A year ago it was seedy, in a charged, eroticized way. I can still see the bedroom, the cracked white plaster walls. The bed with the white sheets, the dirty windows, the dusty palm bushes outside. The blue foil condoms. I loved fucking Pablo so much. I know he loved it, too. He wasn't faking. One time he came without even touching himself, which, let's face it, is not something you can fake. *Why* he liked the sex so much is perhaps another question. Because I think he knew all along what he was doing. That every time I fucked him, I was getting in deeper, no pun intended. But that's the thing about fucking. It's an old cliché, but it may be true. The person on the bottom is really in control. At least that's how I see it with us. When I saw that sweet brown butt I came running just like he'd rung a bell. I was Pablo's dog.

So I'd drive by here sometimes and be wistful. This was the wistful period. I'd drive by here, or by the beach where we met. Or go to Tito's with Charlie, where Pablo and I used to eat. Telling myself it was research. Not that I didn't know those places already, but somehow being there I had a sense I'd connect with something ineffable. Or have a certain breakthrough thought. L.A. geography is funny that way. I associate certain street corners with certain thoughts. Not memories, thoughts. What I was thinking once as I drove down Sunset Boulevard, took a free-flowing right down the easygoing hill of La Cienega. Which happens, I guess, when you spend half your life in a car.

One night at the beach I thought I saw him. The Saab wasn't there, but I thought it was him. Because of the T-shirt, the goatee. So I got out, but then I lost my nerve. I couldn't approach him. I hung back. I wasn't absolutely sure it was him. I'd been fooled before, on the goatee issue. It was dark, and I wasn't wearing my glasses. So I watched. And whoever it was watched me. Then he struck up a conversation with some guy on a bicycle. That's when I decided it wasn't Pablo. He looked chunkier than Pablo. And I couldn't believe that Pablo would react that way if he saw me. That he wouldn't take off. Unless he was sure that he'd beaten me so badly that

I'd be afraid to approach him. To be honest, I'm still not absolutely sure it wasn't him.

But I left. And somehow that was a turning point. In a way, it didn't matter if it was him or not. It might as well have been him, that was my feeling. If it wasn't him, he was somewhere else, doing essentially the same thing. Out cruising. Which seemed very sad, but also made me see that it wasn't my fault, what had happened. That I was ready to settle down with someone, but he wasn't. He couldn't. He had to end it before I found out too much about him. He was afraid that once I did, I'd reject him.

Which is true, if I'd known everything. But I think at this point in some way I forgave him. I finally let go. I mean, I still had this fantasy of running into him at SCA. That we'd get back together. But the incident at the beach made me realize how impossible that was. I *couldn't* approach him, when I thought it was him. A part of me wanted to, but it was as if I were being magnetically repelled. So it was over. You couldn't roll back time. You couldn't put a cliff back up after there'd been a landslide.

I have to tell you, I wish it had stopped there. I wish I'd left L.A. at that point, so that I'd never have heard another word about Pablo Ortega. I really didn't know, I didn't have a clue, about what was coming, or I would've.

I'm sweating. I don't understand this heat today. It's sticky. I hate it when it gets like this. It's East Coast heat. Some kind of tropical condition.

Anyway, I'm outta here. I need the air-conditioner on. I think what I'm going to do, though, as long as I'm here, is take a quick look at the beach. I wouldn't expect Pablo to be down there. I don't think he's into that, sitting on the beach. We never did that anyway. But today, to be honest, anything's possible. I still have this feeling about today, so we'll see.

So anyway, I went through this period of perfect release. It was so perfect that for a while I didn't even work on *Testosterone*. Partially, I was sidetracked, helping Sean with his 'zine. Then I met Frank, the yoga instructor. That didn't last long, but it was still a good thing. A preview of life after Pablo. I still planned to return to *Testosterone*, but the time felt right for a break. I'd soaked up a lot of new information from SCA, and even the incident at the beach—I felt like I might want to use that. But these things have to go through a subconscious process. I don't live it in the afternoon and draw it that night. That's not the way I operate.

But I felt good, that's the point. I felt healed finally, like this new sunny day had begun. I was no longer angry. I could get up and go through whole days barely thinking of Pablo at all. So I should've packed my bags and moved to Portland or someplace. Before I ran into Mark again. That's what happened. As soon as I saw him, I should've turned and ran. But I always realize these things too late, after the scene is over.

OK, I'm at the foot of Windward here. I'm not getting stuck on Speedway again. I'm parking here, I don't care about the fucking ticket. This won't take long. I'm just going to scan the crowd. Back in a minute.

❋   ❋   ❋

Oh, man! I'm outta here. OK, let me get outta here. Come on, get the fuck out of my way! Come on, move it, fuckhead! Come on, goddamn it. Fucking pedestrians.

OK. Man, my heart is pounding. I'm a jacked-up mess. I gotta get outta here. I didn't see any cops. Any of those beach patrol guys in shorts. But I've got to get outta here. This is bad.

OK, I'm on Pacific now. I guess I'm all right. I don't expect a chase or anything. I don't expect to hear sirens. Except maybe an ambulance. I don't think anyone followed me to the car. But who knows? It's hard to tell. You know Venice Beach. It's a mob scene. It's packed down there today, packed.

OK, so this is what happened. I might as well tell you. My heart's still pounding, but I might as well tell you. I think I'm all right. I mean, I'm getting away. Maybe nothing will happen. He might not report it. I mean, he doesn't need it either, right? I just hope I didn't kill him. Not that I'd care on a certain level. I just don't want to be charged with anything.

Calvin. What a scumbag. I mean, I'm sorry he's got AIDS, OK? I wouldn't wish that on anyone. Truly. But here's the thing. That doesn't turn him into a saint. Having AIDS, I mean. It's not like it suddenly turns him into E.T. Although there is a resemblance now, which is scary. He's only, I don't know, forty. But he looks like this wizened E.T. in a wheelchair. E.T. with a little seventies clone moustache. I mean, that's his era. That's where he's coming from. Basic Plumbing. Remember that club? The old sex club? That was his hangout, circa 1981. Licking smegma off the glory holes. That's probably where he got it.

Pablo's best friend. Maybe Pablo's only friend. That was something I noticed, that Pablo didn't have a lot of friends. He had work associates. Names he'd toss out. But Calvin seemed like it in the friendship department. And it always seemed a little creepy, like they were maybe too close. Like he told Calvin everything.

The one time I met Calvin was by accident in a movie line. At the Westside Pavilion. Pablo and I ran into Calvin with a friend. So this was Calvin, this name I'd been hearing. I was shocked and appalled. For some reason I'd pictured him as a snide, blond, dated eighties-preppie. This real estate guy with a Palisades background. I pictured him blond, I don't know why. Instead he was this icky little dark-haired disco-era clone with a sickening Gale Gordon moustache and plastered-down hair like Rupert Pupkin. You know, *The King of Comedy.* So it was instant revulsion. And then he said something to fuck with my head. He said, "Oh, yes, I feel as if I already know you." With this creepy, queeny, overly sticky sarcasm oozing out of his female brain. Like Pablo had told him everything, every single thing we'd ever said or done. So it upset me at the time, at the Westside Pavilion. Wondering how Pablo could be best friends with someone so repellent. It was incongruous, since Pablo wasn't a queen. Or, was there something I didn't know? Did Pablo act a certain way with me, cool and scientific, then turn into a queen with Calvin? When he could let his hair down? Were they two "sisters" who got together and shrieked? Well, I don't know, but I think there are limits to how far in that direction Pablo could go. I don't think he switches genders, for example. We talked about that once. I don't know if he and Calvin talked trash in the true sense, like totally stupid gutter queens. Supposedly, they were honest with each other, "painfully honest." Whatever that means.

OK, I'm coming into Santa Monica. I guess I'm OK.

James Robert Baker

Calming down a little. So here's what happened.

I'm down on the boardwalk, checking out the gay beach. I mean, just standing there, looking out across the sand at all the tanned bodies. And suddenly I'm starting to feel weird and self-conscious. Like I can't really see anyone that well, they're all too far away, but I don't feel like walking out across the sand to take a closer look. Since I don't even know who I'm looking for. I'm not looking for Pablo. I don't expect him to be there at all, so really it's kind of a fishing expedition. But I also feel strange, in the Jim Morrison sense. Like I get a funny look from two guys in Speedos. Like I'm putting out a strange vibe, even though I think I'm acting normal enough. They can't see my eyes, since I'm wearing dark glasses. And I'm dressed appropriately. Baggy trunks, T-shirt. So I don't get it. I don't get what's wrong with me. Unless I'm putting something out that I don't want to. So I feel that if I walk out among the bodies I'm going to attract more attention. Like it's going to be obvious I'm not haplessly looking for some friends. So I decide I don't need that. To have a bunch of airhead muscle queens make me feel like a psycho. And besides, it's probably pointless. So I'm about to go when I see Calvin coming up the boardwalk in his wheelchair. Being pushed by this big fem black guy.

I don't recognize Calvin for a second. I mean, a year ago, at the Westside Pavilion, he was maybe a little drawn-looking, but on his feet and all that. In fact, Pablo never said anything about Calvin having AIDS. But he did talk about Calvin's background, Basic Plumbing and all that, so I kind of assumed he might have it. I mean, according to Pablo, Calvin was so upset by Ronald Reagan's election in 1980 that to blow off steam he went to Basic Plumbing and got fucked by thirteen guys. That's what Pablo told me. Which was strange in itself, a bit of a breach, that he'd tell me something like that about his best friend. He told me other things, too, which I wouldn't tell a boyfriend about my best friend. I think Pablo and I had different concepts of confidentiality.

So anyway, I see Calvin in the wheelchair way before he sees me. This is about to get grotesque, incidentally. I mean, it's not pretty. And I'm not exactly proud of what happened, but I'm not sorry either. So I'm watching Calvin, and I'm kind of in shock, seeing his condition. I mean, just on a basic human level, seeing anyone in that condition. And he seems kind of out of it, rolling his head around like Stevie Wonder, so I'm trying to decide what to do. Like a part of me is saying: Forget it, walk away. But on another level, this is kind of a jackpot, running into Pablo Ortega's best friend. So I feel I can't ignore it. I know if I don't approach him, I'll kick myself five minutes later. So I see it as this challenge, to try and get what I want from him in a humane, compassionate way.

So I intercept him. Or them. The black guy, who's a home nurse or Shanti person or something. He sees me before Calvin does. He gets this startled, scared look, which confirms that I'm putting out something, even though at this point I'm not consciously mad.

Then Calvin sees me, although this isn't clear at first, since he's doing this Stevie Wonder number, with the head-rolling and the eyes. But when I say, "Hi, Calvin," he says, "The cops are looking for you. You're going to go to prison."

So obviously he's still in touch with Pablo, he's up to date, since this is a reference to what happened with Pablo's mother. I'll go into that in a minute.

So this is disturbing, this thing about the cops. Which is not a surprise, but I still don't like hearing what I've already suspected. That there's a warrant out for my arrest. So I'm already starting to cross some weird line. Like if I'm already a criminal, I might as well go ahead and act like one.

But I still say, as calmly as possible, "Where is he?"

And Calvin says, "You're a crazy man. You should be in an institution."

So I say, "Look, I just want to talk to him, OK? Tell me where he is." Which is absurd, of course. Like Simon Wiesenthal saying he just wants to shoot the breeze with Eichmann. So I already know what I'm going to have to do.

Calvin says, "You're insane. You should be locked up."

That's when I snap and grab him by his collar. Pull him up from the wheelchair, which isn't difficult, since he weighs about eighty pounds. I know what you're thinking. Go ahead and be appalled, I don't care. I really don't give a shit. I'm sorry the guy's got AIDS, but he's still a little scumbag. And he's still Adolf Eichmann's best friend, so I have no fucking sympathy for him at all.

So the nelly black nurse is yelling, "Sweet Jesus! In the name of God!" This big humanist shtick.

And I'm shaking Calvin, saying, "Where is he? You tell me where he is."

And Calvin starts coughing, but I don't let him go, even though this nurse is trying to pry me off. I don't know. I mean, I chose to grab him, it was a conscious decision. But once I did, some sort of rage kicked in. So I was kind of in a blackout. Some kind of pit bull state or something. Where I just wasn't going to let go until I got what I wanted.

The point is, I don't know how long this went on. Not too long, I guess. But I was in this strange timeless state. I was kind of aware of people gasping, people looking appalled. But mostly I was focused on Calvin's face, his mouth, which was twisted and prune-like, like Arthur Schlesinger Jr.'s. And I'm saying, "Where is he, where is he?" Until Calvin finally says, "I don't know. He *was* at his mother's. But I don't know where he is now. I don't know."

The next thing I know, I've let him go, because some other guy, a big, bare-chested straight guy, has finally pulled me off. And Calvin is having this total coughing fit, and everybody staring at me like I'm an animal, a monster, since they don't know what's going on, they have no way of knowing. They just see me as some violent psychopath who's gratuitously attacked some pathetic dying man in a wheelchair.

Except not quite. I mean, I think people sensed it was personal. This straight guy, for example. He kind of backed off when he put it together that Calvin had AIDS. I mean, on some level people had to see it was personal, not some senseless random assault. Otherwise I don't think they would've let me get away. Or maybe seeing that Calvin had AIDS was a factor. Like if I'd roughed up a pretty young woman with a brain tumor, if I'd yanked the once-allegedly virginal Kimberly Bergalis out of *her* wheelchair, they would've lynched me from a palm tree. But since it was fag-on-fag... I don't know. But I'm glad I got away.

Look, I know what you're thinking. And I'm not proud of this, I'm really not. But I'm not going to say I'm sorry.

James Robert Baker

Because I don't think Calvin was leveling with me. That's what I think now. I can't believe he doesn't know where Pablo is. They're too close. If I'd had another minute, I could have gotten it out of him.

❊ ❊ ❊

OK, I'm back. Stopped at that liquor store at Ocean Park and Main for a jug of Evian. Man, I'm still sweating. It's this fucking heat. And beating up an AIDS patient takes a lot out of you. I hope he doesn't die. This afternoon, I mean. I hope they didn't have to take him straight to the hospital. If he dies, my goose is cooked. This is not what I intended. He's not the one I want to kill today.

But I'm being dramatic. Look, all I did was grab his collar. I don't see how that could kill him. Anyway, fuck it. I'm not going to spend the rest of the day obsessing about that. That's already behind me. I'm moving on.

I'm on Ocean Avenue now, by the bluffs. It used to be nice along here, you could walk your dog at night if you were a straight couple. In the forties Tennessee Williams blew sailors along here. I read that in his memoirs. People still cruise along here, farther to the north. But along here, where I am now, by Wilshire, it's fucked up. Homeless people, crack dealers, killings. So the straight couples can't walk their dogs anymore.

Right now I'm going up to O.J. Country. Brentwood. That's my next stop. Not that I'm going to actually stop, but I just want to see. In a way, I'm still looking for Pablo's black Saab.

Anyway, I'm calmed down now, so I want to tell you what happened with Mark. So you won't think I'm some psycho who goes around beating up PWAs. Even though I didn't "beat him up," let's be clear about that. But here's what happened with Mark.

This was two months ago, the scene I'm describing now. I went into that Thrifty's at Wilshire and 18th Street [in Santa Monica], and I saw Mark in the store. Standing around, waiting for a prescription. Crixivan, as it turned out. He hadn't lost any weight, though. He was still chunky. I saw him before he saw me, and I thought about ducking out. But at this point I no longer blamed him for setting me up the last time. I'd forgiven Pablo at this point, remember. So I no longer blamed Mark for stirring me up. I also had this feeling I should at least see how he was doing. Some sort of survivor's guilt, I guess, although I find that concept facile. Anyway, I walked over, just to say hello.

So we talked in the aspirin aisle. He was wearing a baggy Jesus Lizard T-shirt. He talked about his health a little. T-cells falling, but nothing serious yet, just skin problems, no major infections. I started to get bummed out, since Mark's an incredibly good artist. I also got this sense that he had something on his mind, which should've been a warning. I mean, I should've taken off while he was still hesitating. But I didn't, and then he said it. He said, "Listen, can I ask you something? Didn't you use to have a dog?"

I said, "Yes. Why?"

He said, "I thought so. I think I saw you with him once. He was a golden retriever, right?"

I said, "Right. Why?"

He suddenly looked at me in this bizarre way. Like a friend who had to tell me my family had been wiped out in a plane crash or something. Tears welling up in his eyes. He said, "I don't know if I should tell you. Maybe I shouldn't."

I said, "Tell me what?"

He said, "When did you lose your dog?"

I said, "What do you mean, when?"

He said, "Was it while you were going with Pablo?"

I said, "Yeah. What are you saying?"

He said, "Well, it looks like Pablo was involved in some sort of animal theft operation. Supposedly, he was the mastermind. He had different guys working for him. Younger science students who'd answer ads in the newspaper, or go to animal shelters. Pretend to be looking for a pet. Then sell the animals to medical research labs. It was quite a racket."

At first I couldn't believe it. I said, "Why would he do that? He made a good living as a coroner." Since that's essentially what he was.

"Not that good," Mark said. "He made a lot more selling animals."

I didn't know, incidentally, the true nature of Pablo's "part-time job"—that he was an assistant coroner or medical examiner—until we'd been going together almost a month. He came in one night smelling of formaldehyde, and when I asked him about it, he told me what he did. He told me very carefully, like he'd had some bad reactions in the past. He even said, "Does that bother you?"

I said, "No. Why should it?" And I tried not to let it bother me, and for the most part it didn't. It was a job; that's how I looked at it. He was a doctor, a scientist, not some pathological ghoul.

I tried not to think about it though—especially when we were having sex. Which wasn't that difficult, since having sex with Pablo always seemed to be this special territory, a place separate from everything else. But sometimes it would cross my mind that the hand on my cock might have been lifting off a skull just a few hours before. So obviously it was something I tried not to dwell on.

There was this, too. Pablo talked in his sleep sometimes. While he was dreaming. I heard him do it a few times, but the only line I remember is this: "Cut off her head." Which is a startling line when you're lying in bed with somebody. But I felt it had to be work-related. Something to do with cadavers. He was dreaming about his job.

Another time we were in bed and he pointed out a vein in my body. Or maybe it was an artery, a major artery, running down my leg. So I asked him about his job, about crime victims. If they got a lot of gang-related deaths, and he said yes. Then he said, "We should talk about this somewhere else. When we're not in bed."

For some reason the way he said this kind of touched me. Like he understood that even though I was curious, I had a much lower threshold, and he didn't want to risk grossing me out, or putting anything in my brain I'd think about the next time we were in bed together. He was protecting my sensibilities. That's how I saw it at the time.

So Mark told me how his dog disappeared. He said, "It never even crossed my mind that Pablo was involved in any way. It was unthinkable. He got along with Sparky. Sparky liked him. Which no doubt made it easy. If he called Sparky, he'd come. He helped me put up signs. Can you believe that? He helped me put up the fucking reward signs."

Mark was angry now, which was strange in itself. He's not like me. He's one of these people who never shows his anger.

He went on telling me how he thought it happened. That Pablo was the one who found the gate open. Supposedly that's how his dog got out. He told me how Pablo reacted. His concern for the missing dog. His hopefulness. "He'll turn up." For weeks Mark kept checking the shelters. All that time, he felt, his dog was either already dead or "in some fucking cage with electrodes in his brain."

Mark said, "I don't have to tell you what I'm going to do to Pablo once I find out where he is. I've got nothing to lose now."

By this time I was in shock. I mean, I'd gone numb. It was so big I didn't know how to react yet. And Mark kept going on in this same deceptively soft-spoken voice he'd used to sneak into my brain the last time. Until finally I interrupted him and said, "Look, I understand what you're saying. That you think Pablo took your dog. Maybe he did. I'm not saying he didn't. But that's not what happened with me."

So I told him how it happened. Or how I thought it had happened. That Tuffy had been attacked and killed by coyotes.

And Mark said, "Did you see him afterwards?"

I said, "Yes," even though I hadn't.

Mark said, "You're lucky." He said fate intervened on Tuffy's behalf, before Pablo could steal him and sell him to the research lab.

He said more, but I only heard parts of it. This was where he mentioned Reese, another ex-boyfriend of Pablo's. Some sort of writer or poet, just a name up to then. He said the same thing had happened to Reese. Pablo took Reese's cat.

I couldn't hear any more. I made an excuse and got out of there. Mark saw what I was doing. He said, "Call me later. There's more."

I threw up in the parking lot behind Thrifty's. Very suddenly, as I started to unlock my car. Like I was trying to reject what I'd just heard. Mark had fed me this poison, and I was trying to physically expel it before it could take effect. That's how I saw it at the time.

But, of course, it was too late. Because this is what really happened with Tuffy. It's still hard to talk about. But I came home one night. It was still light out, actually. It was sunset. And I pulled up, and Pablo's Saab was there. He was inside the house, and the front door was open. At this point he had his own key. So the front door was open, but Tuffy didn't come out to greet me the way he usually did. And as soon as I saw Pablo I knew something was wrong, just from his expression. I didn't know what it was at first. I thought someone had died. I mean, a person. That's how he looked. But then, before he could say anything, I saw Tuffy's collar on the counter. I said, "What's going on?"

And he said, I'll never forget it, he said, "Jesus, Dean. I wish I didn't have to tell you this."

But here's the part, the truly sick part, that still flips me out. There were tears in his eyes. His eyes were brimming with tears. Not because he was attached to the dog. But because he knew I was. That's how I read it at the time, anyway. So he told me that a neighbor had called. One of the yuppies up on Saddle Peak Road. Using the number on Tuffy's tag. To say that Tuffy had been killed by this pack of coyotes.

That someone else, another neighbor, had called the sanitation department. Since it happened in the road. There was all this carnage in the road. So they sent out a truck, but the first neighbor got the dog tag and called. When I heard about the truck, I kind of flipped. Since I saw them do that once in Venice, saw them scoop up a dead dog. Kind of flip it into the truck. So my first thought was to try and reclaim the body, give him a burial. But Pablo talked me out of it. He said he went up and talked to the neighbor, and it wasn't anything I'd want to see.

So I ended up sobbing. And Pablo kind of held me on the sofa, and he was very consoling. And it was strange. I don't want to get into this whole thing about animals right now. Except to say I don't confuse them with people. In theory, anyway, I still think it's much worse when a human being dies. And yet the truth is, I cried more that night over Tuffy than I have over the deaths of a lot of people I've known. Of course, that's a whole other thing: AIDS deaths, how you numb out to those or dole out your grief. But there is this sense that animals are innocent. That's the point I'm trying to make. There's a special kind of innocence. Which you can't always say about people. I don't mean in terms of AIDS. On the contrary. You know how I feel about that. But people can do things that are less than pure. Whereas with animals, even when they're vicious, there's this basic sense of guilelessness.

I don't know. I feel like I'm trying to justify my grief. When maybe I don't have to. It's a reaction, no doubt, to what was really going on that night. Because at the time I tried to feel like: OK, it had to happen one way or another.

When you get a dog, you know that. He'd lived ten years. He'd been this companion through a very empty period. So I felt that if it had to happen, at least it happened when I wasn't alone anymore.

In a way I felt closer to Pablo that night than I ever had, or ever did again. Since a lot of it, let's face it, was about sex. Or sex and some bizarre emotional thing. But that night it was like we suddenly stopped playing whatever weird game we were playing and were just human beings or something. Except of course I know now that even while he was kissing away my tears, he was secretly laughing at me.

I'm on San Vicente now. Where Nicole Brown Simpson used to jog. Coming up to the site of the altercation. The Brentwood Country Mart. That's where I took on Señora Ortega. Actually Mrs. Clarke. Mrs. Stanton Clarke. She married some rich Republican. An Anaconda Copper executive. They live up on Cliffwood, north of Sunset, just a hop, skip, and a bloody glove from the O.J. estate. It took me a while to get their address.

But it's funny. This was two weeks ago. Cinco de Mayo. And I had this idea there might be a party. I'd already driven by the house a few times before then. But I thought, you know, since his mother is Mexican, that there might be a party or something. That Pablo might be there. A long shot, but I figured, why not?

Except just as I pull up, his mother is leaving. Dolores Sanchez, that was her screen name. She was a Latin glamour girl, in the fifties primarily. By the late sixties she was doing those Mexican horror films. I noticed one in the *TV Guide,* on one of those Spanish-language cable channels, 34, 38, whatever it is. *The Aztec's* something. Some body part. *The Aztec's Twat* or something. What's the Spanish word for *twat*? What is this thing they have about body parts? I mean, *Bring Me the Head of Alfredo Garcia*—that's only sick if you compare it to *Mrs. Miniver* or a Merchant-Ivory film. It's part of a great Latino film tradition. I don't think most Anglo critics got that at all.

So anyway, I tail *el madre*. In her black Mercedes 500SL. I get a good look at her as she pulls out of the gate, and she's dressed to the max in this hacienda getup, the combs in the hair, the whole bit. Like the hostess at El Cholo or something. This hard-core *Ramona* look. Like she's clearly on her way to some fat-cat fiesta somewhere. So I'm thinking I'll just follow her, see where she goes. Once I get there, look for Pablo's black Saab. It's a long shot, but he's close to his mother. Very close. Just knowing where she lives is a major coup. Since by this time I'm tracking him. I'm completely playing detective. This is all I'm doing, every day. You see, I knew she lived in Brentwood, but I didn't know her husband's name. Finally, on a long shot, I called SAG and did some fast talking. She hasn't acted for years, but they still had her name in their computer, her address.

So I follow her down Cliffwood, onto San Vicente. Then she turns into the market lot, and suddenly I get this idea that maybe I can trick her into telling me where Pablo is. I suddenly get this brainstorm, that I can pretend to have met her. I'll pretend to run into her as she's walking from her car. "Mrs. Clarke? How are you? Jay. I guess you don't remember. I was a grad school friend of Pablo's. How is he, anyway? We lost touch." Etcetera. All I need is a phone number. I can get the address traced from that.

You see, in fact I've never met her. I almost did once, but it didn't pan out. Pablo and I were going to go up to the house for dinner. Then Pablo got the flu. This was close to the end. Another reason I thought things were actually going well. I was finally going to meet his mother. She knows he's gay, but she's sophisticated. That's what I got. That she accepted it. She was just concerned that I wasn't a psycho, like this guy Ron he'd lived with for a while. That's what Pablo told me. She said, "I hope this new man in your life's not like Ron." He told her, "No, Mom. He's nothing like Ron." At least that's what he said. I don't know what they were doing while they had this conversation. Maybe cutting off Lassie's paws with an electric knife or something.

So I pull into the lot of the Brentwood Country Mart and park across from her, but here's where I make my mistake. She's still sitting in her car, messing around with her bag or something, getting herself together, but I'm started to get hyper. Like she's taking forever to get out of the car, and meanwhile my adrenaline is kicking in. So I want to move while I can still seem casual, before I get so jacked up she'll smell something. So I get out and walk over past the car, like I'm headed for the market. And her window's rolled down, and when I reach the car, I kind of do this double take and say, "Mrs. Clarke?"

She doesn't buy it for a second. I still don't know why. Maybe she spotted me coming up in the sideview mirror and got freaked in general about robbery or something— that's possible. Or maybe it's my eyes. I'd taken off my dark glasses, thinking that would make me look more innocent, less threatening, more sincere. But maybe it has the opposite effect. Whatever, she looks totally horrified and scared shitless, her mouth distorting all over the place, like she thinks I'm a psychotic rapist. She's still pretty, incidentally. I mean, I'll give her that. No spring chicken, but still beautiful, in a fleshy-faced kind of way. Like Linda Ronstadt at sixty.

So I persist for a second, even as the window's rolling up. Acting incredulous. "Mrs. Clarke, I'm a friend of your son's." But I know it's hopeless. And when I allude to Pablo, she goes into this hyperterror state. I think that's maybe when she realized who I was.

Which is strange. Because I believed at the time that Pablo had no idea how intently I was looking for him. Which was naive, I guess. When you're asking people questions, totally playing detective, sooner or later word gets back. I still don't know who tipped him off, although I have some ideas. But at this point I was telling myself: Boy, is he going to be surprised.

But now she's acting like: It's that man! That man who's obsessed with my Pablo! The next thing I know, she's picking up the phone, the cellular phone. The next thing I know after that, I'm at the back of the car, snapping off the antenna.

That's when she panics. I mean, she could've driven off. If she'd started the engine and backed up, I couldn't have stopped her. But she's not thinking. Instead she bolts from the car.

Or maybe she *was* thinking, since there were people up by

the market. She starts to scream for help. That's when I grab her and cover her mouth. I say, "Where is he?"

She was quite an armful. Not a big woman, but squishy. Squishing around in my arms. A ton of perfume. It was strange. I had this sense-memory of my grandmother, from when I was a little boy. These big spongy bazooms.

So she's struggling, and I keep saying, "Just tell me where he is and I'll let you go. I don't want to hurt you."

But when I let her speak, she says, "Why are you doing this? What have we ever done to you? Why can't you just leave us alone?"

She's kind of convincing, and for a second I feel like some totally sick psychopath harassing decent people who only want to lead good, clean lives. Then for another second I wonder if she's somehow innocent. Like she really doesn't know what her son's about. But I don't believe that. Which is why I say, "Look, you fucking right-wing pig. You tell me where he is, or I'm going to rip your tongue out and shove it up your ass."

She starts screaming and scratches me pretty good across the neck. That's when I kind of flipped. And I still don't know why I did this, I wasn't really thinking. Except I couldn't bring myself to hit her, to hit a woman. So instead I pulled down her dress. With both hands, I grabbed the front of this low-cut dress she was wearing, and also her brassiere, and yanked down hard, so that her huge tits flopped out.

Well, she howled, mortified, but I considered this action lightweight, and still do. To me, this bitch is Eva Braun. Knowing what I know now, I have no sympathy for this foul cunt at all. I cut her no special slack because she's a woman and Latina. People are responsible for their own vile actions irrespective of race or gender. I judge her the same way I would judge any straight white man.

On some level I also knew that I was sending Pablo a message. I mean, I realized at a certain point that she wasn't going to tell me where he was, and even if she did, by the time I got there, she'd have alerted him. But by doing something like this, I felt, even cool, dispassionate Pablo the scientist was going to blow a fucking gasket. This action would bring him to me.

I mean, it's no secret how Latino men feel about their mothers. Not that I don't feel the same way, even though I'm Anglo. I would certainly defend my mother's honor if someone called her a whore in public. There'd be a fistfight at least, you can be sure of that. But I don't think I'd go into vendetta mode. That's the difference. I'd react at the time, then I'd get my mom home and say, "Forget it. Those morons aren't worth it." I wouldn't organize a drive-by. So I was certain I'd done the one thing that would smoke Pablo out.

I was starting for my car when Mrs. Clarke said to me, "You're going to die." The way she said it made me look back. I mean, on one level it was hopelessly corny. I think a part of me was fascinated by the cheap drama of it. It was like something from one of her horror films.

She said, "You're going to die. In a car crash on the freeway. My son, he has the power."

Just like that. So campy it should've been a joke. Which in a way it was. But my skin still crawled. She's also doing this sign, this hokey hand gesture, like she's laying on a curse. She's holding up her dress with the other hand.

I couldn't just walk away. I fired back. I said, "Fuck you, cunt. You don't scare me with that Latin mumbo jumbo."

She said it again. "You're going to die. It will happen soon. You will burn in a car on the freeway. My son, he holds your soul in his hand like a trembling bird."

This woman had something, I'll tell you, to bring off shit like that. But she did. Because something about it scared the fuck out of me. Not that I believed it was true. But she believed it. For what that was worth. That's what scared me, I guess. It's just not very pleasant knowing someone's praying with all their might for your death.

It was also chilling because up to then I'd been able to dismiss all this Palo Mayombe shit Reese had tried to tell me about as speed-freak paranoia. But I don't want to get into all that yet. I'm on Cliffwood now, coming to the house.

This is crazy in a way, if there's a warrant out for my arrest. But Mrs. Clarke won't know this car. I was in Charlie's Honda when all this happened at the market. Obviously, she didn't get the license or they'd have tracked me down by now.

But I just want to see. I'm still looking for that black Saab. Who knows? He could be having a Saturday lunch with Mom. Tostadas Benji. Dipping body parts in salsa.

But here's the house. Big ranch house back behind a gate. There's her Mercedes. She's got a new antenna. It's a beautiful house. Elm trees, the whole bit. *Muy* WASP. There's the gardener's pickup. But no Saab. Oh well. I'd better get out of here, before she comes running out across the lawn with a new, better curse.

Hey, baby, I'm still alive, and I've been on the freeway a

whole bunch lately. I'm the one with the magic. I'll be back later, *mamacita,* with your Pablo's head in a box.

❉   ❉   ❉

OK, a new dispatch, a new direction. Right now, I'm taking a lunch break. Got gas at the Arco on Barrington, snagged a sandwich. I'm parked on Sunset at the 405, finishing this dry chicken sandwich. Wish I had a toothpick.

OK. It's time to get going. North on the 405, down into the Valley. Let's roll up these windows fast. OK, we're on the road again. We're moving. Good.

You know, this thing about the warrant surprises me. This thing Calvin said, about there being a warrant. Maybe it was crazy, but I never really thought Dolores would call the police. Especially after her mumbo jumbo number. But maybe she wasn't taking any chances. If the magic won't get him, the LAPD will. I don't know. Or maybe somebody called the cops at the market and she had to tell them something.

Or maybe she's just into respectability. Like a Mafia family gone legitimate. In Chile she'd order up a death squad, but here she plays by the rules and dials 911. I don't know.

But it's scary because I spent the next five days after the market waiting for Pablo to show up at my house. I really figured he'd blow. He'd want immediate revenge. I pictured him showing up at the door with a couple of friends. With a couple of young students from his animal theft ring. I didn't expect him to be armed. I didn't think he'd want to kill me. He wouldn't want to throw everything away by doing that. But he'd be seriously into teaching me a lesson. He'd be into having his friends hold me down while he beat the fuck out of me for what I'd done to his mother. Except that would never happen. He'd die on the front porch.

You know how my house was. The bedroom upstairs overlooked the front porch. I was going to blow his head off while he stood at the door.

So it's strange, if there was a warrant, why the cops didn't show up during that time. It's scary, since I wasn't sleeping very well. I mean, there could've been an accident. I was pretty jacked up, maybe even slightly crazy. I might have shot a plain clothes detective on the front porch, thinking he was Pablo. Especially at night, if I wasn't wearing my glasses.

It's a legal firearm, though, so they couldn't have got me on that. They could right now, of course, which is one reason I've got to drive carefully today. It's one thing having a gun in your home for protection. But having one under your car seat is another thing. Then it becomes a concealed weapon. If there is a warrant, I'm already in trouble. I don't need to be charged with anything else.

It's funny though. In a way I'm still blown out that he tried to kill me. I mean, I can see him burning down my house to hurt me, to fuck me over. As a symbol, a warning, a very serious warning. And he could've done that if he'd wanted to. Watched the house from Saddle Peak Road, waited till I went out. But doing it at three A.M., he obviously meant to trap me and kill me. It's funny, it doesn't make sense, and in a strange way it just surprises me. It almost hurts me, as crazy as that sounds. To know he hates me enough to try to kill me. Because I don't think I've done any-

James Robert Baker

thing. Except rough up his mother. But I'm not the guilty party here. I'm not the monster, he is. But, of course, if he's Mengele, I'm Simon Wiesenthal. I'm one of his camp experiments who didn't quite die. I've got his tattoo on my arm, and now I'm closing in on him. He knows that. He may even be a bit panicked now. That's why this may get messy. He's not going to give up quietly. He's like a mad cornered South American dog.

TAPE 3

OK, a new tape. A fresh new tape. I want to go back to the period right after I talked to Mark at the Thrifty's. That was five weeks ago. It's the most crucial period, between then and now.

I can take my time here, since I'm going down into the Valley now. I've got thirty smooth uninterrupted minutes. Or longer, not so smooth, if the Ventura Freeway's jammed.

I'm playing sex addict now, incidentally. That's what I'm doing. I'm trying to think like a sex addict, which isn't that hard to do. It's not a great leap, like trying to think like a lesbian. I got into this while I was eating lunch. That's why I shut off the recorder for a while. I needed to think on a deeper level, without talking. I had to become William Petersen in *Manhunter*. This really hot, somewhat older guy putting himself into the mind of a killer. Of an emotional serial killer, a sexual psychopath. I had to sit there and soak up the humid atmosphere and feel my cock jerk in my swim trunks, imagining what I would do on a day like today if I were Pablo Ortega. That's why I'm headed for Griffith Park, which is a good half hour away. So I can stretch out now; I can take my time narratively as I come down to the Ventura Freeway. I want to take my time here. I feel that I need to remind myself that there are still decent people in this world. There are still people who don't think tenderness is weakness or a joke.

So after I ran into Mark at the Thrifty's, I did nothing for several days. I mean, I waited three or four days before I called him. I got mad at him again, mad at myself for listening again. I tried to think that Mark might be getting demented from HIV, manufacturing this bizarre delusional scenario about stolen pets. I mean, rationally, I just couldn't see it. Even if Pablo had been involved in something like that, why would he risk everything by stealing the pets of people he knew? It didn't make sense.

Except of course it did. The greater the risk, the greater the thrill. And I knew he liked thrills. And what would be more in keeping with his emotional sadism?

So I was getting mad again, but it wasn't a clean anger yet. I was mostly in shock, appalled and sickened. Filled with a kind of moral disgust, if these charges were true. I didn't want to get enraged again, not when I'd finally put it all behind me. I didn't want to have to kill Pablo. For all the obvious reasons. So when I finally called Mark I had an agenda. I wanted to catch him in a slipup that would let me off the hook.

That didn't happen. Mark was calm and rational as we talked on the phone. But I began to realize that the source for a lot of what he was saying was this guy Reese. And when I asked for Reese's number, Mark got edgy. He finally gave me the number, along with a lot of explanations and disclaimers. I understood why as soon as I got Reese on the phone. He'd been up for three days. He sounded fried and hard-core paranoid. Mark had warned me he was "something of a speed freak." When Reese started going into this Palo Mayombe stuff, I cut him off.

I was ready to throw out the case after that. I felt Mark was sincere, but I decided he'd been infected with Reese's paranoia. Basically, I decided that no pets had been stolen. I mean, animals disappear all the time, right? Cats especially. That's what I got from Reese. He lived in a raunchy neighborhood, it was an outdoor cat. Who the hell knew what happened to it? As for Mark's dog, Sparky, he was a beautiful dog. And friendly. Somebody might have snagged him on the boardwalk and kept him. And with Tuffy, up in the hills there'd always been the threat of coyotes. That's a real danger when you live up there. So I slipped back into this precarious denial. I mean, the one thing I could've done to find out if Pablo had lied about Tuffy I didn't do. I didn't go up and talk to the neighbors who'd supposedly found the body.

This was my last attempt to stop everything. To keep the dam of new information from bursting. Because Reese, before I cut him off, told me things I was not ready to deal with. Things about Palo Mayombe. About their love of putrefaction. The way they use body parts in their rituals. How they sacrifice animals.

I think a lot of the reason for this final stab at denial was still sexual. I didn't want my erotic memories contaminated. I didn't want to know I'd been turned on by a vile, animal-killing ghoul. That I'd been starring in a forties women's picture, a Fritz Lang picture, *I Married Mengele,* with me in the Joan Bennett role. Going to bed with Gregory Peck circa *Spellbound.* Waking up with Gregory Peck in *The Boys From Brazil.*

And there'd been no proof. At least none that I'd seen. According to Mark, the animal theft ring had been busted a few years ago. A kennel out in the Valley had been raided. Some students arrested, but Pablo wasn't there. Nor was he identified as the mastermind. But the story was there in the *L.A. Times* if I wanted to look it up. I didn't.

Reese supposedly had evidence too. Photos from one of Pablo's ritual sites. I didn't want to see those either. I mean, on some level I knew it was all true. I already knew I was going to have to kill him. I was just trying to find a way around it.

But when Mark called me and said, "There's someone you've got to talk to," I didn't resist. Or get angry when he said he'd already given the guy my number.

So a while later "Will" called. Not his real name, but the name he used. We talked briefly and agreed to meet the next day at Cal Arts. He was calling from a pay phone, in case the call was traced. He sounded bright, confident, and I could tell he was gauging every nuance of what I said, wondering if I was part of a setup. So it was strange, like setting up a meeting with a terrorist. Which I guess to some people is what he is. If certain animal rights groups, like PETA, are aboveboard and official, the group Will belongs to is like the IRA.

I agreed to meet him in one of the quads, an area with trees and concrete tables. I got there early and waited. It was noon, and I noticed a men's room across the quad, which I quickly realized was one of the campus cruising spots. I could tell from the guys going in and out, how long they were taking, the way they checked each other out. I caught a few looks, like they assumed I was there for the same reason, positioned so I could watch. All these really young guys, young art queers, which was discouraging. Since I always think of tearooms as part of an older era of closet-case oppression. So it was troubling to see how much it was still going on, even when gay men had all these other options, other ways of meeting. But of course it wasn't about meeting. It was about fast sex. Or reptile-brain conditioning. That's how I felt. Like I was watching a Pavlovian experiment. Lab rats in baggy shorts, Doc Martens, goatees.

The scene also made me feel almost nostalgic for the relative innocence of a few months before. When I'd thought that Pablo's worst offense was being a sex addict. I'd looked for him then in different Westside tearooms. Not obsessively. But sometimes if I had nothing better to do, I'd drive by different places I knew about and look for his car. Hoping to catch him in the act. At first, when I was angry, wanting to humiliate him. Hoping to catch him hunkered in a stall, pants around his ankles, masturbating like a sick pathetic creep. I wanted to see the look on his face when he saw me. I wanted to say, "You sick piece of slime. You threw away what we had for *this*?" I imagined that seeing him in that setting would burn away the last of my residual desire.

Later, after SCA, when I was "compassionate," I'd sometimes extend the scene. I'd catch him; he'd cringe in mortification under my withering gaze. But as I left, he'd catch up with me. He'd break down, sobbing. Admitting he was sick, that he needed help. Begging me to forgive him. "I didn't mean to hurt you, Dean. I was scared. I knew if you found out about this, you'd reject me."

Usually in this scenario, I'd forgive him. If his tears and remorse seemed sincere enough. I'd take him back, and he'd start going to SCA again, to deal with his compulsion, and we'd live happily together, grateful we'd found each other again. We'd grow old together. Living in New Mexico. Of course, in this fantasy he'd still be negative.

I was thinking about all this at Cal Arts when Will came up and introduced himself. Not who I expected. To be honest, I was watching for a geeky guy, a dork. Which is maybe unfair, but that's the impression I had of animal rights guys, just from a few public access shows I'd seen.

It's funny, but until this all happened, it was not an issue I'd thought about much. I mean, I love animals, I always have. But I had mixed feelings about animal research. I felt that some of it was necessary. In a way, I still do. What I'm saying is, I don't think I'm sentimental about animals. I know some people are, that's why it's a hot issue, an emotionally charged issue. And sometimes these animal rights people I saw on TV went too far. When they talked about liberating lab rats, I'd think: Wait, where do you draw the line? What next? Don't swat a fly? I mean, my feeling was, some animal research was probably necessary. When it came to testing AIDS vaccines, definitely. Testing makeup was another matter. Sticking lip liner in rabbits' eyes, that was clearly cruel, especially when there were other ways to test it. But basically I was not very knowledgeable about the whole issue. For a male homo, it seemed pretty low on the list of compelling issues, with AIDS at the top. That's the other thing I'd think: How can you get so upset about animals when so many *human beings* are suffering? It seemed like a luxury issue for privileged straight people or something.

And in a way that's what I first thought about Will. When I thought he was straight. Which he may be, I'm not sure anymore. But when I first saw him, I decided he was this young straight artist, and I also found him attractive. So maybe I went into this hypercritical mode as a defense mechanism.

He wasn't as young as I'd expected. I'll say he was thirty. But he's one of these people where it's hard to tell. Blond hair and Irish skin that was never meant to be fried in California sunlight. So his skin was kind of prematurely aged. But he seemed young in certain respects. He seemed intelligent, cautious, but not jaded. Paint-splattered clothes. He wasn't currently a student there, he said. He'd graduated a few years before. He didn't tell me much more than that about himself, and I didn't ask. I still had this feeling I was making contact with the Bambi faction of the Baader-Meinhof gang.

He led me down into what I'll call the bowels of one of the buildings. The bowels of Cal Arts. On the way he asked me if I was a cop or law enforcement official. I told him no, and he smiled, like he was sorry he had to ask. I understood. I wasn't sure how much Mark had told him about me. But I got a sense I could be up front, that he wasn't homophobic.

He led me into this cinder-block room, which was almost like a police interrogation room, with just a table, some chairs, and a VCR and monitor. He stuck in a cassette, and I braced myself, having some idea of what to expect.

He said, "I have to tell you, this won't be easy to look at."

James Robert Baker

He was right. Because even when it's fiction, in a Hollywood film, I have a real problem with cruelty to animals. I can't take it. It's the one thing I can't take. Sometimes, if I see it coming, I'll stop watching the film. If I can see the setup. Like in *Revenge,* remember? That piece-of-shit Kevin Costner film? That's how that was. As soon as you see that he's got a beautiful dog, you know it's going to get snuffed eventually. I just have a real problem with that sort of thing. Which may be sentimental, I don't know, since it does involve a certain double standard. I mean, *people,* I can see people get killed in various elaborate, sadistic ways, and it doesn't bother me intrinsically. But there's this sense that sometimes people have it coming. Especially in movies, it's often set up so they're not guiltless. They're the bad guys. Or even when good people get killed, you know it's just drama, it's this worked-up thing, so maybe you're affected in varying degrees, but it's not this thing where you feel that someone's trying to cut up the tenderest part of your soul. So knowing how I felt about this sort of thing, I really braced myself. Since this wasn't fiction, I wasn't being manipulated by a cynical director, this was real.

Will showed me two tapes. Or parts thereof. As much as I could stomach. The first one was bad, but I was able to maintain some distance. This was a tape Will's group had made of one of their lab break-ins. So it was this smeary home video of a corridor, then the room where these animals, dogs and cats, were in cages. And it was bad, the animals looked scared, but it wasn't as bad as it could have been. There weren't any electrodes screwed into their heads. Will said they were part of a deprivation experiment, which sounded pretty appalling.

Like one of these things where they got a grant to scientifically prove something that was obvious to begin with. That if you isolate an animal long enough, you'll drive it insane.

Will said this lab was one of Pablo's biggest customers. But of course there was no proof of that in the tape. I mentioned this, and Will stuck in the second tape and said, "You might want to brace yourself. This is something they shot themselves."

He said they found the tape when they raided one of Pablo's kennels.

As soon as it started I knew it was Pablo. It was him in the foreground. You couldn't see his face, but I recognized his arms and the T-shirt he was wearing. This Jesus and Mary Chain T-shirt he was always wearing when we went together.

You couldn't see his face because the camera, which seemed to be mounted on a tripod, was aimed at the dog in the cage. A beautiful but terrified-looking collie.

I still find it very hard to describe this. But what happened is this. Pablo opened the cage door, speaking softly and soothingly to the dog. And then without warning he stabbed it in the eye with a scalpel.

The dog didn't die right away. It banged around, bleeding and whimpering. But here's the worst part. And here's how I knew beyond any doubt that it was Pablo. He laughed. The same way he'd laughed the one other time I'd heard him laugh. He *shrieked.* He shrieked with delight.

I said, "I can't watch this."

Will shut it off.

I said, "I have to get out of here."

What I wanted to do was leave, get in my car and drive, get as far away as I could. I think Will sensed that. He kept talking to me as we went back outside, like he didn't want to me leave, he'd shown me the tape for a reason.

So we sat outside in the sunlight. Will got me some coffee. I couldn't say anything for a long time.

Finally I said, "How could he do that? How could anyone do that?"

And Will said something I'd already kind of thought of. Although he said it better than I probably can right now, so that it didn't sound racist. But Latinos do have this different feeling about cruelty to animals. I know that's a blanket statement. I know there are Latinos who undoubtedly love their dogs. I'm not saying they're all sadists. That Gabriel Garcia Marquez likes to take a writing break and step out back and stab Lassie in the eye. I'm not saying that.

But there are the bullfights. Which I know are graceful and all that, but still quintessentially sadistic. Unfair. That's the thing. It's not a fair fight. That's what's sick about it. I can understand competition, the thrill of winning. If it's a fair fight. But killing a bull or stabbing a dog in the eye, that's some other thing altogether.

Or swerving your car, going out of your way, to run down a dog in the road. Then giggling. Which is something that carloads of young Latinos get a kick out of doing in here in L.A. Call me a racist if you want to, but it fucking happens. That's why it's taking a great effort on my part not to think all Latinos are sick.

Then Will started talking about Palo Mayombe. And because it was Will, not some paranoid speed freak, I listened. He said,

"We know that some of the animals were being used for that."

In other words, what Pablo didn't sell to the labs, he sold for sacrificial use in Santeria and Palo Mayombe rituals.

"And I'm sure he used some of the animals himself that way," Will said. "We know he's into Palo Mayombe."

I said, "I can't see how he could believe in something like that. It's so crackpot and superstitious. He prides himself on being this coldly rational scientist."

Will shrugged. "Mengele was a scientist. And he believed in a lot of crackpot stuff."

Then he started telling me about the *nganga*, this pot or cauldron they use in Palo Mayombe. That's where they put the sacrificed animals. As well as body parts, human brains. "They like fresh corpses," Will said. "So there's a lot of grave robbing. Of course with Ortega that wouldn't have been necessary. Since his job gave him access."

At this point I had to get out of there. But Will walked me to my car, giving me his recruiting pitch. He said that Pablo was very clever. Even though his operation in the Valley had been raided, there was no hard evidence against him. The tape, Will said, was useless, since it didn't show Pablo's face. Since it had been obtained illegally. "The cops see *us* as the criminals," Will said.

He said Pablo hadn't quit his coroner's job. "He was let go," Will said, "to avoid a scandal. They suspected him of stealing body parts, even though they couldn't prove it."

He was still in L.A., Will believed. Pablo felt invincible. "That's what Palo Mayombe is all about," he said. "When they perform these rituals, they feel spiritually protected."

That's why he was certain that it wouldn't be long before

Pablo was up to his old tricks again. If he wasn't already. Will wanted me to help find Pablo.

"If you could talk to his ex-girlfriend," Will said.

I said, "His ex-what?"

So he told me about Anne, like he thought I knew Pablo was bisexual. Which I did, kind of. At least I knew he'd had relations with women in the past, the same way I had. But I didn't really think of him as bisexual.

From what Will said, I realized Pablo must have been with Anne after me but before Brice. They'd approached her, Will said, but she was still ambivalent about Pablo. They felt she knew where he was, but she was protecting him.

"When we tried to tell her what he was about," Will said, "she literally slammed the door in our faces." He thought I might have better luck, since I could approach her on other grounds. As another of Pablo's emotional victims.

The way Will said this, that word *victim* again, kind of set me off. Not just *being* a victim, but having other people know, even virtual strangers like Will.

Then he said, "Look, don't blame yourself. This guy is evil. He seeks out people who are basically decent and trusting."

For some reason the way he said this made me wonder if he could be gay. Or, I'll put it like this: At a certain point I forgot that I was talking to a straight guy. And I wondered if I'd forgotten because he wasn't.

I told him I'd have to think about it, about whether I could help him. So we left it at that. But I thought about him a lot as I drove home. I thought about how maybe it wouldn't be a bad thing at all to get involved with him in some protracted Pablo hunt. We could be like the Hardy Boys or something.

Two homo Hardy Boys. Like it would get to be late and he'd stay over one night, and we'd crawl into bed together, still wearing our boxer shorts. We'd be tense at first, until one of us broke the ice. Then we'd start making out ferociously, getting hard-ons, etcetera.

I mean, I knew I was slightly infatuated with him. Bedazzled, smitten, whatever dorky word you want to use. You would be too, if you saw him. But in a certain sense, it wasn't even sexual. Or just sexual. It had more to do with what he represented. An intelligence that wasn't snide. A virility that wasn't sadistic. I liked the idea that he broke the law. That he was willing to do that, toward a beneficent end. Instead of breaking the law in a cheesy way, like a thief or a drug dealer. I liked the idea that he cared about animals without being fussy or ridiculous. That was a big part of it.

So I had these fantasies that we'd track Pablo down together, in the process becoming boyfriends. We'd get the goods on Pablo, attend his trial in the Criminal Courts building, watch him be taken away to prison.

But I already knew it wasn't going to happen. That if anyone went to prison, it was going to be me. For killing Pablo Ortega.

That night in bed I thought about the way Pablo had held me the night Tuffy was supposedly killed. When in fact he was across town in a cage somewhere. Destined for a lab or, more likely, one of Pablo's own rituals.

I thought about the feeling I'd had—which, of course, I'd dismissed at the time—that even as he'd comforted me, Pablo was secretly laughing at me.

He'd said a few things that night that were too much even

for me. He said something about Tuffy being in "doggie heaven," which even in my grief struck me as kitsch and cloying.

He was just seeing how much he could get away with, how far he could take it. Knowing what he knew, that must have given him a real sense of power. An indescribable thrill.

I remember, that night after talking to Will, lying there in the same bed where Pablo had robbed my soul, thinking: Whatever you did to my dog, that's exactly what I'm going to do to you.

I haven't talked to Will since we met at Cal Arts. Which is too bad in a way. The more I think about it, I'm almost certain he's gay. I wish I could call him right now. He might even talk me out of this. He gave me a number where he could be reached. But I lost it in the fire.

❖ ❖ ❖

All right, a new adventure in a new part of town. Actually, an old part of town. I'm getting off at Los Feliz now. Griffith Park is just minutes away.

It's vile over here today. Vile skies, vile air. Urine-colored skies. The color of [Fassbinder's] *Querelle*.

This is where Pablo met Reese, here in the park. That's how I know it's one of his haunts. At least it was at one time. He might not come here anymore, afraid of running into Reese. Reese has been looking for him longer than anyone.

But I still have this feeling that I'm going to find Pablo today. So I can't afford to ignore any hunch.

Anyway, Anne. This always seems like a Costa-Gavras film, when I think about it. When I met Anne in Pasadena and she told me her story, it was like a Costa-Gavras film with silent flashbacks. Some here, some in Chile. I understand why. A lot of my visual impressions of Chile are from [Costa-Gavras's] *Missing*. Even though that was actually shot in Mexico.

Anne's a doctor. In her mid thirties, Jewish, beautiful. I'll tell you who she reminds me of. Marianne Williamson. That's who she looks like. Thin, beautiful. She comes across as smarter than Marianne, though. Not that Marianne's stupid. Considering all the AIDS-vulture loot she's raked in with her *Deep Thoughts* best-sellers. You know how I feel about all that New Age teddy-bear-with-an-AIDS-ribbon shit. But Anne's not like that. She seems like what she is, a brilliant research scientist. Like Sigourney Weaver should play her in the movie version of this.

I called her at Cal Tech. I said, "Look, I don't know if Pablo ever mentioned me—"

And she said, "Yes, he did." She sighed, this big resigned sigh, like she'd been expecting me to find her. So she agreed to meet me at a coffeehouse in that upscale part of Old Town Pasadena. As if she felt it was her duty to do it or something.

Even before I met her and she described how she'd met Pablo, I'd realized who she was. That she was in fact this unnamed woman doctor Pablo had mentioned while we were going together. They'd met at some conference at Cal Tech, then they'd gone out for drinks.

Pablo described what happened next like this: "We had a few glasses of wine and got pretty loose. And she admitted that she was sex-crazed the same way I am. Which most women won't admit to."

It's worth pointing out that "sex-crazed" was his wry, cleaned-up alternative to "sexually compulsive." Like saying "sex fiend," which is sardonic, instead of "sex addict," which isn't.

So we were having dinner at Crocodile Cafe when he said this—he said, "I really wanted to fuck her. And she was ready. And I could have rationalized it, since she was a woman." Since at this point we were supposedly monogamous.

I'd said, "Why are you telling me about this?" Even though I knew. He was bragging. He wanted me to know that women also thought of one thing when they looked at him. That he'd almost fucked a woman. So it was this weird, competitive macho thing, even though we were boyfriends.

He said, "I just wanted you to know I didn't do it. Even though I wanted to."

Which, of course, was a totally feeble and unbelievable reply. But I let it go. I felt he was just trying to stir me up, get me jealous or something. And it worked. As I recall, once we got back to my place that night, I fucked the shit out of him.

As it turned out, he had fucked Anne. That's what it sounded like when she told the story. They'd met at this conference and gone out for a drink, then back to her place. She didn't seem that sex-crazed, incidentally. Not that you can tell. Not that I can tell, with a woman. Or maybe after what happened with Pablo, she's switched off her "Easy" sign. Of course, we're drinking lattes in this crowded coffeehouse, and she's this brilliant scientist, so you wouldn't expect her to be flashing her snatch.

She told me Pablo's version of what happened with us. That I'd become possessive, with flashes of unexpected rage that had caused him to end the affair. Then I'd "stalked" him, he told Anne. "Like *Fatal Attraction*." I was still out there somewhere, looking for him, he'd told Anne. This explained his frequent moving. From Venice, back to the Wilshire District briefly, before moving in with Anne.

The thing with me was so bad, he'd told Anne, that it had soured him on gay life for good. Always bisexual anyway, he now longed for a healthy, uplifting relationship with a woman. With Anne.

She read my mind and said, "We took the AIDS test together. I wanted to be sure that he was still negative. He told me you were."

I said, "I am." And couldn't bring myself to tell her I hadn't known that when I was with Pablo. Or ask if she knew that she'd been shacked up with a tearoom queen. I wasn't sure how much she really knew about all that. If Pablo's version where they'd swapped sexual sleazebag confessions was accurate. If it was, I decided, she was not nearly as sane as she looked.

"We were monogamous," she said, "as far as I know." As far as she knew.

She seemed nervous. She said, "I have to tell you, this is really the worst thing that's ever happened to me."

I said, "I know. What did he do to you?"

"What did he do to me?" She looked scared. Then she said, "He lied. He manipulated me."

She said, "Look, he's done some truly vile things. I didn't know about it until the end, I swear to you."

I almost asked if she meant the animal theft operation, but something told me that wasn't it. I also had a suspicion that might have been the real way they met. That she was buying animals from him for her research at Cal Tech. I had no reason to suspect this, I didn't even know if her research involved animals. It was just a feeling.

I said, "What do you mean? What vile things?"

"In Chile," she said.

I said, "When was he in Chile?"

"The same time I was," she said. "In '87."

She was down there with a human rights group, she said. Helping to organize opposition to Pinochet at a time when that was still extremely dangerous. So I began to understand why she'd found Pablo especially irresistible. She probably already had a thing for Latino men. Chileans especially.

"It was always odd," she said. "He told me he'd been a medical student at the university in Santiago. Comparing notes, we realized we'd been at the same street demonstration that summer. One the Army had disrupted with water cannons. But the way Pablo remembered it wasn't quite right. It felt like a kind of pathological lie."

She was afraid at the time to call him on it, she said. "I think I was always afraid of him on some level," she said. "Not that he ever lost his temper with me. Or abused me in any way. Until the end. But there was always a sense that he could."

I asked her what happened at the end.

"We went to a party," she said. "A fund-raiser in Beverly Hills. For Amnesty International. A lot of Hollywood people were there. Ed Asner. Martin Sheen. Ed Begley Jr. And one of my best friends, Isabel, who'd fled Chile. She hadn't met Pablo before that. As I introduced them I could tell something was wrong. Isabel pulled me aside as soon as she could and said, 'I know that man. He worked for DINA.' The Chilean secret police. 'He tortured people.'"

Of course, Anne's first response was incredulity. Her friend had to be mistaken. So they peered out of the kitchen, or wherever they were, so Isabel could take another look at Pablo, who was eating cheese dip and chatting it up with Isabel's husband.

"It's him," she said. "I'm sure of it." He'd been a doctor at the detention center in Santiago where they tortured people. Isabel had seen him there while she was in custody. She hadn't been tortured herself, but she feared him; everyone did. He was notorious. Bet you can't guess what his nickname was. Which of course he thought was cool. A compliment adding to his sexy, evil mystique. "Mengele."

That didn't surprise me.

"He knew something was wrong as we drove home that night," Anne said. "I knew it was true, but I still didn't want to believe it. I mean, you know, I thought I was in love with him. So once we got home I told him what Isabel had said. Still hoping he could convince me it was a mistake. But I knew from the way he responded that it wasn't. He said, 'She's crazy. Your friend's insane.' But he was changing, changing personalities. His eyes. He looked like a trapped animal. I was suddenly very afraid. He saw that. Which clearly excited him."

At that point, I remember, a waitress interrupted us. Once she was gone, Anne said, "So...he raped me. Then he told me if I called the police, he'd come back and kill me."

She said she believed him. So she didn't call the police. She said, "The worst part, worse even than the physical assault, was the depth of the emotional betrayal."

I wasn't sure what she meant, so I asked her. She hesitated

a long time before she said, "Well, early on, we shared some very private things with one another. Pablo told me...I don't know if this is true or not. But he told me he'd been molested as a boy, raped by his father. Repeatedly. He felt that was why he'd become gay, to the extent that he had. He didn't feel that he was intrinsically gay, as some people seem to be. In his case, he felt it was a kind of pathological acting-out. The way he presented this, I was very touched. He was weeping. So I told him that I'd also been raped. That I knew what he felt. You've got to understand, I don't usually tell people this. I'm not someone who goes around announcing that I was once a rape victim. But I trusted him."

I asked if she knew where he was, if she had any idea at all.

"Why?" she said, kind of staring into her latte. "So you can kill him?"

I said nothing.

She gave me this hard look and said, "If I knew where he was, I'd tell you."

※ ※ ※

Well, I'm in the park now. Definitely in the park. I'm going by the West Hollywood section. That's how I think of it. There are two cruising sections. And this one here is where the white clones go. I mean, the old clones and new clones. They park along here and hike back into the hills.

It used to be different. A few years ago. You used to be able to go up along this road that went around the crest of the hills. There'd be guys parked along the road in alcoves. But that road's closed now. Ostensibly because of fire danger. But no doubt to discourage the cruising. The road was still open when I came up here once and jacked off with an Italian-looking guy. That was right before Pablo saved me from all that.

I don't see his Saab. Again, assuming he's still driving that. But I don't feel like getting out, hiking back into the hills. Trying to find the action. I don't really feel like doing that. I'm going to turn around up here. Check out the other side of the park.

Here's a young guy with a sexy goatee. And an ACT UP T-shirt. That's a bit dated. Here's a muscle boy. Nice pecs. Too bad he's going to be dead in a few years. But maybe he doesn't care. AIDS is one thing. But sagging pecs—now that's a true tragedy. Gay men are like replicants now. Some of them. A lot of them. It's like they don't even want to live past thirty. Like what's the point? Being gay is a young man's game. At least in this arena. Which makes guys like this kind of abject. This guy up here who looks like Vidal Sassoon. Leather-faced guy getting out of his BMW tanning machine. The last living disco clone. Reptile brains always bring 'em back for more. He must like rejection.

So I'm going to case the other side of the park. The multicultural side, that's how I think of it. The dinge-queen sector. It seems like mostly black guys. But also Latinos, a few Asians. Saw a hot young samurai over there once. Shirtless, in shorts, hairy legs. Should've fucked him.

But anyway, I'm not finished with the Anne story. There's a twist. A major reversal, you could say. Three days after I saw her, she called me.

She said, "I've got to tell you something. This is difficult.

But everything I told you the other day about Pablo...none of it was true."

So I was blown out, to put it mildly. And I sensed that in fact she was lying *now*.

I said, "What do you mean by everything?"

She said, "Just that. He was in Chile when I was there. That was true. But he didn't work for the secret police. That's not true. He didn't rape me. In fact, we never had an affair. Not for lack of trying on my part." Here she choked out a "breezy" laugh. "Do you understand what I'm saying?"

"I guess."

"Look, I was mad at him. I was in love with him. In love or obsessed, whatever you want to call it. I wanted to hurt him. I felt that he'd hurt me. But I know the truth is, I only hurt myself."

For some reason I said, "Then you don't have a friend named Isabel?"

The panicked way she responded told me she did. She said, "Look, I'm thinking of *you*. That's why I called. This isn't easy for me. In fact, it's humiliating. Listen to me." Here for the first time she started sounding real. She said, "You must forget Pablo. Don't let him destroy you. You've got to forget him. That's not easy, I know. He has his magic. But it's what I'm trying to do, I'm trying to put him out of my mind before he destroys me."

That was it. She hung up. No point in calling her back. She'd shut down. I understood. She'd told me too much. Maybe she *was* thinking of me. Maybe I should've listened to her advice. Maybe I still should. But I can't. It's too late.

His magic. I wasn't sure what she meant by that. But I

assumed she meant it figuratively. Not literally, the way Reese meant it. Reese is my next stop.

But right now I'm passing the Observatory. Lots of buses, Japanese tourists. This place is ruined for me now. Ever since that fucking Paula Abdul video. That *Rebel* rip-off where she ran around here with Keanu Reeves. That's all I can think of now, instead of James Dean. Stumpy Paula Abdul trying to act like Natalie Wood. She's lucky she drowned when she did. Natalie Wood, I mean. Too bad Paula didn't drown. Except I guess she has—careerwise, I mean.

We came up here once. Pablo and me. Just to look around. My idea. It didn't seem to mean that much to him. I mean, he knew *Rebel Without a Cause,* but it didn't have the same reverberations. An age thing, maybe. Not that I was into James Dean at the time. In the fifties, I mean. I was still in diapers. But I discovered him later. In the seventies, I guess, when I read that biography. So we walked down to where the knife fight took place, but Pablo seemed bored. The telescope didn't work either. I lost a dime.

We took the straight way in and out. I didn't want to drive through the cruising section. Didn't want Pablo to know I knew about it. He didn't say anything about it either. We were boyfriends at this point. We even did stuff like hold hands in the car.

I'm going into multicultural cruising land now. And here's an unusual guy. An intellectual. Reading a book under a eucalyptus tree. Interesting. Twenty-five, I'd say. Messy brown hair, glasses. REM T-shirt. An old one too. The *Document* cover.

I'm passing him now. I think he's looking up. But I don't

want to make eye contact. I'm shy. But here's the test. In the rearview mirror. Will he still be looking at my car? Knowing I'm looking to see if he is. Yes. Yes, Jesus. He's very interested. He put his fucking book down. Like he just saw the love of his life.

I shouldn't be so cynical. But I am. He's still looking. But now I'm going round the bend. And he's out of sight. History. Oh, well.

OK, here's somebody parked in a beat-up Honda. What's this look? Long hair, mustache with mutton chops. Like what's-his-name, Metallica. James Hetfield. Heavy metal blow job? Maybe someday, but not right now.

OK, here he is. Jesus, this guy's a fixture. [Names a well-known gay author.] He's always up here. In his little yellow bikini. Putting on baby oil. Look at this guy. How old is he now? Sixty? What's he trying to prove? That he can still show off his body? That's it, I guess. That's exactly it. I mean, he's still in shape. He's still got a good body. For a sixty-year-old man. But his is not a teenage face. That's probably why he's wearing shades. To hide the riot of wrinkles. Oh, well. Look, it's fine with me. It seems sad, though, in a way. He's given his whole life to this place.

So I'm coming down to the parking lot now. And there's Danny Glover. Big black guy. He's looking at me. Like he wants to stretch my sphincter. Not today, Dan. Go stretch Mel Gibson's.

I like this area, though. I prefer this side of the park. It's looser. Hear that music? Can you hear it? Someone always has a radio going. Or a boom box. Which makes for a looser atmosphere. More erotic. Less tense. It's more of a party atmosphere over here. I'm turning into the parking lot now. There's some sort of weird retro ambience here. Like the fifties. Black guys and skinny Southern fags with dirty-blond hair. A *City of Night* feeling. Or even going back further. To the thirties or forties. Like one of those Paul Cadmus paintings. Where everybody's cruising with bulging crotches, all juicy-looking, sexed-up, aching to fuck.

And there's a Saab 900. But it's not Pablo's. Unless he painted it gray and had it aged. Here's another black guy. More my type. Not too huge, bearded. He looks sensuous. I'd like to kiss him. In a perfect world, that's what I'd do. I'd stop and get out and walk over, and we'd start making out. Big sloppy tongue kisses. Then I'd pull out his hard cock and suck the come right out of it. While everybody gathered around and whacked off, drenching us.

But jizz isn't what it used to be. Neither is sloppy tongue kissing, for that matter. So all I'm going to do is talk about it today.

A world's been lost, though. And I'm still not sure whose fault it is.

Here's a character. Man, this guy is scary. Native American guy. Shirt off, nice bod. But his face is giving me chills. Like that guy in *Body Double*. The guy with the power drill. I'm not into that today.

OK, I'm making a U-turn. And what's this? It's the REM guy. In his red Peugeot. Has he followed me? It's possible. It's entirely possible. I'm slowing down. I don't know why I'm doing this. I'm not really interested but...I'm curious.

OK, he's pulling over. He's parking. I'm just sitting here now, idling. I'm just curious. I want to see what he's going to do. He's about a hundred yards away. OK, he's getting out. Oh, Christ, he's got a dog. Looks like a spaniel. I didn't see the dog before. He's letting the dog run off into the grass.

OK. He just looked over. He knows I'm here. I think he followed me. He's calling the dog now. OK.

Oh, man. He just peeled off his shirt. He's got a really nice little body. Not built-up but tight. Nice pecs. A really nice bod. Firm. Compact. Nice little butt in loose faded jeans. I think I'm in love.

OK, he's sitting down under a tree. Oh, shit. You know what I think he's reading? It's that Rimbaud book. Rimbaud's collected works. With the pale blue cover. I think that's what it is. I'm almost sure of it.

Oh, man. He just looked over again. But just for a second. OK, I get the picture. He's playing shy now. He knows I like that. So it's my move.

I'm not sure what to do.

I mean, what can you tell about someone from a hundred yards away? I can tell that's he got a really nice little body. That he likes REM, that he's reading Rimbaud, that he's got a dog. He's an animal lover. He's intelligent. He may not be infected. He could be my dream. But I'll never know unless I go over and talk to him.

And here's the thing. I've run out of places to look. At least for now. There are other places I can look later, much later tonight. But for now this is it. I'm not going to drive all over L.A., checking every tearoom in the city.

And here's something else. I think I'm having a moment of clarity. I think that maybe I'm being given a chance to deflect my course. I don't know. It still makes a lot of sense to kill

Testosterone

Pablo. When I think about it. But maybe I shouldn't. Maybe I've thought about all this too much. You could make that case.

I don't know. I'm trying not to read a lot into this. So that whether or not I go talk to this guy turns into a major life decision. But unfortunately that's what it may be.

He doesn't know it. How could he? He has no way of knowing what I'm up to today. But I know.

I mean, I know I could be all wrong about this guy. I'm turning him into this big symbol just based on a few details, a few meager bits of information. He could turn out to be stupid or boring. Or unappealing. I haven't even seen his face up close yet.

But I'm pretty sure he's appealing. I'm pretty sure he's the kind of guy I've always wanted to meet. He's smart. He's an animal lover. He was into REM back before they got big. He looks bohemian. Even his car. This faded red Peugeot. Almost rust-colored. I like everything about this guy. Including his hot little body. I think I'll be sorry if I don't at least see.

If it doesn't work out I can always go ahead and kill Pablo as planned. That's how I see it. That's a good way to look at it. That takes some of the pressure off. It's not like I'm making this big life decision.

OK. I've got to do it. No more hesitation. If I don't act now, he might think I'm not interested. He could leave, and then where would I be? This could be my last chance. It's crazy, I know. A lot to lay on somebody. But this guy could save me. Without even knowing it. This could be the start of something. Three months from now, when we're living together, I'll tell him what I almost did today.

I'm going over now. I'll be back, maybe. Or if things work

out, who knows, I might erase all this. Throw these tapes in the fire.

※ ※ ※

OK. Let me get out of here. Before he realizes what I did. Before he sees that I snagged his crank.

Let me explain. That might be ambiguous: *snagged his crank.* Sounds like I cut off his penis. That's not it. I didn't do that. He had a nice one. But I didn't want to cut it off. Quite the contrary. But it didn't work out. It wasn't his fault. I spooked him. I blew it pretty bad.

OK, I'm coming to Los Feliz. No sign of him in the rearview mirror. I'll still feel a lot better once I'm out of here. He might not come after me, though. He doesn't seem like the type. Pretty mild-mannered for a speed freak.

Of course, that's an unfair assumption. If you can believe him. He said he took it to study. His name was Steve. USC grad student. Twenty-six.

So this is what happened. I approached him. We talked. It was Rimbaud, incidentally. That's what he was reading. I was right about that.

His dog's name is Genet. Cool dog. Friendly. So we talk for a while. He says he's taking a study break. Which freaks me out for a second. Since that's what Pablo said the night we met. But he doesn't seem like Pablo. He can smile, for one thing. He can laugh. He's got a sense of humor. He's appealing. Not cute exactly, which is just as well. I'm not into cute. A plain face that will probably age well. Green eyes, nice mouth. So we talk for awhile. Which is cool. He doesn't seem all sexed-up, like he wants to duck back into the bushes. Which is good. Because the longer we talk, the more I start thinking I'd like to spend some time with him. Go back to his place. Fool around all afternoon, into the night. Which would keep me from doing the other thing.

But he's so casual I start wondering if he's interested in me. I start feeling insecure. But he keeps talking. He isn't trying to blow me off. Then I say something about the heat, about feeling depleted, since I feel like I'm not being sparkling enough conversationally. And he says, "Well, I've got something that might pep you up. Would you like to do some crystal?"

So for a second I think he means shooting it, so I kind of freak. Thinking, you know, about bloody syringes. And I'm also kind of shocked, since he seems like this intelligent student, going to USC and all that, not some scummy crank queen. He must see my expression, because this is when he explains that he's not really into speed as a rule, he just got some for studying, and he mentions snorting it. So I think, even though speed doesn't really agree with me, it might not be a bad thing, since the fact is, I'm fading. The heat, plus the Jack Daniel's I drank with Brice, is starting to give me a headache. So I say OK and we get into his car.

So we snort some lines off his Rimbaud book. And the stuff's pretty good. It packs a rush, even though it feels like it's been cut with battery acid. But as soon as it hits, you don't mind the pain. I haven't done speed in a long time, so it doesn't take much to affect me.

So that's when he starts coming on. We're sitting there in his Peugeot, both kind of feeling this rush, and he runs his hands up my leg, under my trunks. Which I don't mind. I get a hard-on. He gets one, too, and pulls out his cock. Which is nice. Not huge but very succulent-looking. And I kind of want to blow him, but he starts blowing me first.

Except then I get nervous. I mean, we're parked some distance away from anyone else, but it still seems pretty brazen. Not that anyone here should care in theory. But I still think, you know, what if there are vice cops around. So I stop him and say, "Why don't we go somewhere?"

He says he lives in a dorm at USC, we can't go there. And I don't really want to ask him back to Charlie's, since I'm sleeping on the sofa and Charlie's due home today. So for a second I'm really bummed and even think of suggesting a motel, except that seems so heterosexual. Getting a motel room. Meanwhile, I'm losing my erection.

Then I say I need a cigarette. But in fact I'm spacing out. Speed does this to me. It doesn't make me speedy, turn me into Robin Williams or something. It turns me into this space cadet. I turn into a zombie. So we both light cigarettes. That's one good thing, he smokes too. And he doesn't seem that disturbed that I want to take a break, if that's what it is. But he leaves his cock out. It's kind of gone half soft. But at one point when I'm looking at it, he makes it twitch and says, "You like that?" Like he's into this total porno thing and wants me to get into it, too. Like he wants me to blow him. And again I almost do. Like it's tempting. He's got a real nice cock, which looks wild in the sunlight, veiny. So I'm thinking I could just chow down, kind of lose myself in this total porno escape trip. But I still don't like the setting, the lack of complete privacy. And I also realize we haven't discussed anything at all yet about HIV.

Then my ears start ringing, like I've taken too much aspirin. That feeling. So I think maybe I've done too much speed. I feel light-headed, almost nauseated. I lean my head against the dash and he says, "Are you OK?"

And for a second I feel really paranoid. Like I don't know who this guy is, which of course I don't. But it goes beyond that. It's almost this sense that he's not even human. My head is so loud it's like I'm alone.

But I say something like, "I'm in trouble."

And he asks what's wrong. And that's when I start to cry. Which completely blows me out. It's so sudden. It just happens. I start sobbing. And then I tell him, I try to tell him, what's going on. I try not to get too specific, thinking that will freak him out more. So I just say, "This guy did something to me. Something really vile. I feel like the only way I can get back my soul is to kill him. But I'm not sure if I'm doing the right thing. I think I may be insane."

I know I'm blowing it, that there's only one way he's going to react. But I don't care. I don't even want anything from him at this point. Not sex, not a blow job, not even understanding. I just feel like I have to tell someone what's going on. Maybe I even want to see his reaction. Like a reality check or something.

So of course he says, "Look, I can't handle this."

By this time he's put his cock back in his pants.

I say, "I know. Look, you seem like a cool guy. I like your dog too. Be careful."

He says, "You should get help." And gets out of the car. Like he hopes it will encourage me to get out, too. Which I do. But first I notice the speed on the divider. This little baggie of crank. That's when I snag it. Which is weird. I'm not usually a thief. It's completely impulsive. I just figure I'm going to need it more than he will.

So that's kind of it. He's calling his dog at this point. Trying not to look at me. Like he's scared, he's spooked, just hoping I'll go away. So that's what I do. But as I walk to my car, this black guy looks at me, the guy I saw earlier who looks like Danny Glover. He stops and stares since I've got tears on my face. Like he's wondering what the fuck happened. It's not something you usually see up here. Tears on someone's face.

※ ※ ※

I'm back on the freeway now. The Golden State. I'm going to see Reese. That's where I'm headed now. Up to Montecito Heights.

It's funny, but I feel like I'm back on track now. Hate to put it this way, but like I'm following my destiny. Instead of resisting it. I'm not saying that's good or bad. It's just how I feel.

So I guess it's time to really get into Reese. Which is a whole story in itself. I mean, I'd talked to him just that once, on the phone, after Mark gave me his number. But after I talked to Anne I called him back and said, "I think we should meet. I want to know what you know."

He'd said OK. Then he'd said, "Look, I know you think I'm crazy, so I want you to do something on your way up here. I want you to stop by Pablo's old place in the Wilshire District and talk to his ex-landlady. I think it might mean more if you hear certain things from her."

So I did that. I'd never known Pablo's Wilshire District address, never been able to get it, but Reese gave it to me. It was on Rossmore a block below Melrose in that strange, well-kept sector where everything looks like a 1930s comic book version of swank urban living. You know, buildings with doormen. Fifth Avenue west. The place where Pablo lived didn't have a doorman, though. What it did have was a creepy faux-chateau look. It's a look I hate. Although this was probably as good as that look ever gets. It wasn't kitsched-out like a West Hollywood apartment building called the Versailles or something. It was hardcore thirties and well-preserved.

The landlady was Hungarian. A Hungarian chain-smoker. I told her I was a psychic, as Reese had instructed. That was the only way she'd talk to me, he said. I had to tell her I was trying to find someone last seen with Pablo. That I needed to enter his former apartment, to absorb his psychic energy, like a bloodhound being given a scent. All this was Reese's idea. I'd resisted at first, but he said it was the only way. The landlady believed in all that shit.

He was right. I said my piece at her door as she studied me with rheumy eyes. Then she said, "Wait here. I get the key."

As we rode up the elevator to the fourth floor I asked her how long Pablo had lived there.

She said, "One year. I tell you something. I knew he was evil the first moment I saw him. But he hypnotized me. That's what I think. His eyes."

She avoided mine.

I said, "What was he like as a tenant? Did you see him much?"

She shook her head. "He had his own stairs in the back."

She glanced at me. "Sometimes late at night he would come in the front way. With the men."

"The men?" I wasn't clear what she meant.

"Young men. Thin. No hair. Like Dachau prisoners."

"You mean, singly?" I asked her, since I still wasn't clear. "With one man at a time?"

"Sometimes. Sometimes more than one." She gave me a leery look. "I try to mind my own business. I'm an old woman. I've seen many things, I've lived a long life. But others complained. The couple downstairs. The sounds woke their baby."

"The sounds?"

We'd reached the fourth floor. She didn't say anything.

She unlocked the door, switched on the light. The apartment was empty. White walls, polished hardwood floor, faint smell of fresh paint. Quite a view through the windows over the treetops looking west across the city.

"I spoke to him about the sounds," she said. "But once my eyes met his, he controlled me. He had the power."

The same line Pablo's mother would use two weeks later. "My son, he has the power."

I kept wanting to ask her what these sounds were, but couldn't bring myself to do it. Fucking sounds, I assumed. The breathless cries of thin young men having their prostates massaged.

She sniffed the air. "Do you smell?"

I sniffed. "You mean the paint?"

She shook her head. She said, "Last summer it became so bad, you could smell it in the hall."

"What kind of smell?" I said.

She said, "Death. It was the smell of death."

She stepped to the window. For the first time I noticed that all the windows were wide open, every one. As if they'd been that way for as long as the apartment had been empty. Which was over a year.

She said, "I called my brother. Together, we entered. Here," she indicated the main room, "all was normal. But back here..." She led the way to the hall. "Come, I show you."

It was a two bedroom place. At the first bedroom she switched on the light. This room was also empty, freshly painted. "Here we found his things."

"His things?"

"Chains from the ceiling. The swing." I assumed she meant a sling. "Over there, a stocks. Ropes. Tools of torture." I noticed she was not stepping into the room. "On the floor," she said, "the dirt of the toilet. Do you understand?"

"I think so."

For a second I hoped that was what she'd meant by "the smell of death." But I knew it wasn't. She stopped at the next bedroom door.

"You turn on the light," she said. Like she didn't even want to reach into the room.

So I switched on the light. And I have to tell you that my skin crawled, even though there was nothing there. It was the same as the other bedroom. Repainted, refurbished. Except the floor didn't look quite right. It had been partially refinished and didn't quite match.

She said, "Here we found the dog."

Well, I quaked. "The dog?"

"There." She pointed to the wall. "Before the altar. His throat was cut. Dead for many days."

I was reeling. "What do you mean? What kind of altar?"

"Idols," she said. "Made of plaster. Evil saints. And a pot. A large pot. Filled with dead animals. Blood. I can't tell you any more. I became sick."

I said, "What kind of dog?"

"A large dog," she said. "Yellow fur."

So that's when I knew. Since she was talking about a year ago, right after Tuffy disappeared.

I said, "Did you call the police?"

"No." She looked scared. "Not then." She started back down the hall. "Come. I show you."

From the living room, she pointed to a cupboard in the kitchen. "In there. We found the jars."

"The jars?"

"Two jars. One held a brain. The other, a penis."

"You mean specimen jars?"

She nodded. "It was then, as my brother examined the jars, that he came in."

"Ortega?"

She nodded. "He went into a rage and hit my brother. He said to my brother, 'If you speak of this, I will kill your sister.' He looked at me and said, 'Do you understand? I will cut off your head.' He said, 'I know you have grandchildren. I will kill them too.' Then he took us downstairs, where he continued to threaten. In my apartment he used the telephone, speaking in Spanish. Soon there was a knock. At the door he spoke to someone in Spanish. For two hours he held us there. I feared for my brother. He is diabetic. Finally he left us. We were so frightened we waited until the next day to call the police. By then there was nothing. Ortega and his friends had taken the shrine, the dog, the jars. Only the smell remained. The smell and the chains and the toilet dirt."

Well, after that I'd needed a breath of fresh air. I was still very shaken when I got to Reese's.

He said, "Did you talk to Olga?"

I said, "Yeah, I did. I think it was my dog that she found."

Reese smiled a little and said, "It's a good bet."

He smiled a little because he knew he didn't have to convince me anymore. Then he explained how Palo Mayombe worked. That to put a curse on someone, to steal their soul, you had to make a sacrifice. So that's what Pablo had done with each of our animals. Reese explained it a certain way. How the animal embodied certain vulnerable emotions because of the nature of pets. Since if you loved your dog or cat, this transference occurred. I'm not using the right terms, but Reese explained it a certain way. So that if you believed it all, it made sense.

Not that Reese believed it at that point. He knew all about it, he'd done all this reading, so he understood it. But he didn't believe it actually worked. But Pablo believed it, of course. That's why he did it.

Reese was not exactly what I'd expected. I was expecting more of a punk, or an aging punk, since he'd been part of that Theoretical crowd. From the early eighties. One of the last of the old One-Way crowd who wasn't dead yet. In fact, he said he was still HIV-negative.

But he looked kind of bookish, with longish parted brown hair, round glasses. Like he could've been a schoolteacher or something. His place was filled with books, too. This old stucco house on Montecito Drive.

He was tweaked, but early on in a run. Not schizzed-out or paranoid yet. He was still capable of a sharp, speed-freak reaction, though. When I mentioned Anne, for example.

"That vile cunt," he said. "Fraulein Mengele." Which seemed strange to say about her, since she was Jewish. But he meant, of course, that she tortured animals. In a sense confirming my earlier fear. If what he said was true. He said she conducted sick psychological pain experiments at Cal Tech. He said, "You're lucky Pablo used your dog in a ritual. At least those deaths are fast. When they kill *animals,* anyway."

So he painted this picture of Anne as the she-wolf of Cal Tech. I wasn't sure how much to believe, since Reese was so over-the-top, you couldn't help but feel he was focusing a lot of his anger and residual jealousy on Anne. Because it became apparent that he'd gone through the same post-Pablo transitions I had. He'd gone through this big "suffering romantic" period right after Pablo dumped him, writing a bunch of poems about their affair. He showed me this chapbook called, simply, "Pablo."

"It's all shit," he said, tossing it aside. "Drivel."

It was over a year, Reese said, after Pablo had abruptly ended their affair, that he realized what had happened. What had really been going on.

He said, "I thought it was just me. That I was fucked up or a masochist. That there was something wrong with me that I couldn't quit longing for him. Then I saw this book."

He showed me this dog-eared nonfiction crime book called *Buried Secrets* [Edward Humes; Dutton, 1991]. He opened it to the photo section and showed me a picture of this young, fine-featured Latino guy. Good-looking, I guess. What most people call *handsome*. Although his hair was a little too perfect and he wore gold chains on his hairy chest.

"Recognize him?" Reese said.

"No."

"Pablo never showed you the photo in his wallet? Of his first great love?"

"No."

"No," Reese said. "Maybe he wouldn't. He showed it to me before this book came out."

Reading the flap copy, I saw that the book dealt with the notorious Matamoros gang. I had a sketchy memory of the story from when it broke in 1989. I remembered that this Mexican drug gang had kidnapped an American college student in Brownsville, Tex.: a gringo medical student down there on Easter break. They'd taken him back across the border and murdered him. Then their place, this weird ranch, had been raided and the Mexican cops had dug up all these other bodies. I remembered something in the news about a "devil cult" or "Satanism." Or, in Spanish, *narco-satanicos*. None of which, as the book points out, are really accurate. Palo Mayombe has its own deities. It's not satanic in the cliché heavy metal sense. It's this Afro-Caribbean religion kind of off to the left of Santeria.

And this guy in the photo, who according to Reese was Pablo's "great love," was Adolfo Constanzo, the cult's leader.

Reese said, "Read the book. You'll see. They were boyfriends in Mexico City in 1987."

I said, "But Pablo was in Chile in 1987."

"Who told you that?"

"Anne."

123

"She's a vile, lying pig."

"Is Pablo mentioned here?" I said, already looking in the index.

"No. But he was there. His mother and stepfather have a house in Cuernavaca. She's part of it, too. Pablo's a mama's boy. His mother introduced him to Palo Mayombe when he was a child. The same as Adolfo. There are lots of parallels. You'll see that when you read the book."

Which I did, later. Or most of it. It was next to my bed the night the house burned down. But that first night with Reese, I was there almost six hours. And he told me so much that the book was in some ways redundant. Of course, in Matamoros they'd been sacrificing *people*. Like they'd started with animals and moved up to human beings. All the bodies the cops dug up were sacrificial victims. So inevitably I asked, "Do you think Pablo's killed anyone?"

"I think he was part of it," Reese said. "In Mexico City. That's where they started killing people. They killed a drag queen. I think Pablo was there for that."

Then he said the line that put me away. He said, "I know for a fact he used his ex-boyfriend's brain."

I said, "What?"

"This guy Mike he was seeing before me. A film student. Pablo told me about him. How Mike was unstable. Brilliant but possessive, so Pablo felt smothered. After Pablo ended it, Mike stayed obsessed with him. He followed Pablo. Pestered him. Pablo finally got a restraining order. Then, several months later, Mike killed himself. Pablo said he didn't know about it. Until Mike's body came in."

"He performed the autopsy?" I said.

"Yes. The way he described it was almost touching. He was

so devastated, he said, that he shut down. Went into automatic. It was only afterward that he broke down and sobbed. Which I almost believed. Almost."

I couldn't help picturing *myself* on the table. Pablo pulling back the sheet to reveal me.

"He took Mike's brain," Reese said. "For his *nganga*. I suspected it. That's why I reported it. That's why they fired him. That confirmed I was right."

OK, I'm coming to Avenue 43. Man, I hate this freeway. The Pasadena Freeway. You know how the exits are. If you don't have good brakes, you're dead.

OK, I made it. I'm off the freeway. I'm in the Latino neighborhood now. It's a poor neighborhood. I think there's some resentment. Against the yuppies up here on Montecito Drive. It's not all yuppie. Reese is not a yuppie. But there are Westec signs. Audis, BMWs behind security fences.

So anyway, I saw Reese a few more times. We talked on the phone a lot. We played detective together, which was strange. He's kind of the ultimate authority on Pablo. He was almost scholarly about it. In a kind of demented way. Which would scare me at times. Realizing he'd devoted four years of his life to this. Like Hitler's biographer. Or, more to the point, like Simon Wiesenthal. And it got strange when we talked about sex. About Pablo's sex habits. Which are extremely wide-ranging. The ostensible purpose was to come up with places to look for him. But at times it still felt prurient. Or vicarious. Not that Reese was jacking off on the other end of the phone. But there was still something weird about it. Or maybe I just felt some envy. That Pablo was out doing all these things without any regard for anything at all. I mean, the part of me that's a soulless sadist was envious. I think everyone has that part. The part that likes the idea of doing anything at all no matter how brutal or selfish or sick without any conscience. That's what Pablo's about.

There was only one time that Reese and I talked explicitly about killing Pablo once we found him. Or rather, about me killing him. It was right along here, by the radio towers, one day when we went for a walk.

We were talking about a cruising place in West Hollywood, an alley Pablo knew about. "If you got him there," Reese said, "you could use a baseball bat. They'd think it was queer bashers."

We discussed other ways. But for some reason I got tense about being so explicit. Like I didn't want to talk about it, have a conversation Reese could quote, if something went wrong. If he freaked out in some way. Maybe I sensed something. Because he did freak out.

The last time I talked to Reese was the night of the fire. He called me and said, "Look, I can't see you anymore. I can't be a part of this. It's over."

This was after I'd roughed up Pablo's mother, of course. And he'd seemed very quiet when I'd told him about that. So I wasn't completely surprised.

Then he said, "Look, I've seen someone. I'm all right now. I've been exorcized. If you want, I can give you his name."

I laughed, which I guess was the wrong thing to do. I said, *"Exorcized?"*

He said, "I'm going to hang up now. But call me if you change your mind. It's the only way out of this. I'm free now. Before I was doomed, like you."

OK, I'm here. There's his car, an old black Toyota. I'm parking now. OK. Let me collect myself. Man, my heart is pounding. I'm pouring sweat, Jim. It's hot but not that hot. I am seriously tweaked.

Which is good, I guess. This is a long shot though. Even if he knew right where to find Pablo, he probably wouldn't tell me now. Except for this. I'm not really into taking no for an answer. If I think he knows something, I'm going to get it. If I have to beat it out of him, fuck it out of him, I don't really give a shit. These days it's the same thing anyway. OK, I'm psyched. I'll be back.

TAPE 4

OK, I'm back, and this is a new tape. Wow. Let me light a cigarette. I think I've got another pack here. Yeah, good. OK. Fuck. I'm trying to digest this. So here's the thing. Reese is dead.

Man, what time is it? OK, four. I'd better get going. I don't know how late this place stays open on a Saturday.

OK, let me turn around up here.

So here's what happened. I go up to the door, which is open, OK? And the TV's on. So I call Reese's name and when he doesn't answer, I step inside. Check the backyard, the bedroom. So clearly he's just stepped out or something. Gone next door. I know he knows the two gay guys next door. So I wait.

Maybe ten minutes pass and I'm sitting there on the sofa. The TV's tuned to the Disney Channel or something. *Old Yeller*. Which gets to be difficult. It's a kitsch film, OK? That's no secret. But it got to me when I was a kid, and it's getting to me now. So I change it to MTV.

A few more minutes pass, and I think about checking next door. I'm pacing around by this time. Then I notice a bottle of mescal in the kitchen. Half empty. I don't think Reese will mind if I take a hit to calm down. So I do, come back out with the bottle. Sit back down. That's when I notice his AA Big Book on the coffee table. Which I never knew about before, that he'd been in AA. He'd never mentioned that. But he was. He was sober six years or something before he met Pablo. Afterward he started drinking again and got back into speed.

That's what Stan told me. I heard someone coming in through the kitchen and thought it was going to be Reese. But it was Stan, who Reese had mentioned as a friend, this concerned, long-suffering friend.

But this is the first time I've met him. He's this big Jewish guy who looks like that guy in *Eraserhead*. I mean, his hair's all frizzed-out in this psycho Gumby style, and he's got this weird kind of insane-looking baby face. He asks me who I am and I tell him, and he says, "Oh, right. Reese mentioned you." He talks like Truman Capote.

I kind of sense that something's wrong and when I ask him where Reese is, he says, "Reese committed suicide two nights ago." Then he adds, "If you want to call it suicide. I'm not sure if that's the right term."

So I ask him what he means, and he says Reese went to this sex club looking for Pablo. Someone had told him they'd seen Pablo there. So he went there on Thursday night. He was found in his car by the club the next morning. He'd overdosed on pills and mescal. So many pills that it was obviously deliberate. But nobody knew what really happened. If he saw Pablo at the sex club, if they had a conversation or a confrontation or what.

"But I have a feeling that's what happened," Stan says. "I told him not to do it, that it was too dangerous. Pablo knew what to say to destroy him. He knew all the soft spots. But Reese wouldn't listen. I think he thought he was strong enough to save Pablo now."

I ask about Reese's exorcism—that's where I'm going now, incidentally, to see this guy in East L.A.—and Stan tells me Reese saw this guy, Hugo, who's like a white witch or something. There's a Spanish word for it. *Curandero*. That's it. He's a *curandero*. So Reese saw Hugo and got himself exorcized. And for about a week, Stan said, Reese seemed OK. Except not really. Like it was desperate. This big religious fervor type thing. Like he was manic. When he heard that Pablo had been spotted at the sex club—when some wonderful friend told him that—he took it as a sign. That he was meant to go into the pit of hell and "rescue" Pablo or something.

So that's it. That's all I know really. Except I have this address for Hugo on Cesar Chavez Avenue. But I don't expect a whole lot from this guy. One thing I know, I'm not shelling out any cash for some crackpot exorcism. Not unless he has a better version than the one he performed on Reese.

Basically I'm just killing time until the sex club opens.

✻ ✻ ✻

OK, another pit stop here. I'm at the market down by Avenue 43. I got a Diet Pepsi. My mouth is still dry. I need to check out the Thomas Guide, find out where I'm going.

I don't think I'm reacting yet. To this thing with Reese. This thing called death. Maybe I can't, I'm too jacked up. Or maybe I am reacting. Maybe *this* is my reaction. Because, let's face it, this is where you have to say: "It's murder now." Because that's what it is. Any way you slice it, whether they talked on Thursday night or not, Pablo killed Reese. I'll bet they did, though. I'll bet they talked. I'll bet they had a nice little chat at the sex club. I really want to know what Pablo said. What he said that broke Reese and made him kill himself. Was it just one line? One highly compressed remark? That's one of the things I'm going to find out before I kill Pablo Ortega.

❊ ❊ ❊

Want to hear something sick? I'm on Cesar Chavez Avenue now, incidentally. Just got off the freeway. I needed some time to think. But here's the sick thing. I just played this Jesus and Mary Chain tape. Like my thoughts were starting to freak me out, so I shoved in this tape to get out of myself. And I still really like them, even though, after X, they're Pablo's favorite group. But there's this one song, "Coast to Coast," that gets me really jacked up, and I was playing it a lot when I first met Pablo. When I had all these sort of weird kitsch fantasies, which I knew were impractical and not based on real life. But I still enjoyed them, the same way you'd enjoy a romantic movie as a guilty pleasure.

So I started seeing Pablo and me in the future again. This kind of ridiculous, hokey sci-fi future. Like it's the year 2024 and we're living in a solar plate-glass house in New Mexico or something. For some reason, New Mexico always seems like the future. I think we talked about it once. Not going there ourselves, but just about the tricultural aspects. So we'd be living in this house with a view of the insanely orange buttes and mesas, and we'd be old men—or older men—but we'd still have good, if somewhat leathery, bodies. And Pablo would have won a Nobel Prize for an AIDS cure or something. And maybe I would have, too, since by then graphic novels would be legitimized as high art. That's it basically. We'd be in this humming solar house in vaguely futuristic clothing. We'd both have silver hair. Pablo might look like Gabriel Garcia Marquez, except not as puffy in the face. We would've been together for thirty years.

It's crazy to be affected by that. It's like being moved by a Douglas Sirk movie. Except maybe that's OK. Maybe it just means I'm still human. That a part of me still wants that kind of stability with someone.

So here it is. Hugo's for Hair. That's right, this guy's a hairdresser. When he's not doing exorcisms, he's saying, "Shake your head, *chichita.*"

I'm in luck. A spot right in front. Oh, man. This is a scene. I'm looking through the windows. I'm censoring myself. I'm trying not to make snide Anglo observations about *chola* women in tight jeans and spiked heels. With hairdos that haven't changed since Ronnie Spector.

OK. This looks colorful. I'll be back.

❋ ❋ ❋

Oh, man. I don't know. This is strange, Jim. This is bad. I think I'm flipping out.

OK. Where the fuck am I? OK, I'm heading west, I guess. On Figueroa. Yeah, right. There's the downtown skyline. Fine. I don't know where I'm going right now. It doesn't matter, I guess. Fuck, the sun's in my eyes. This guy has me very freaked out.

So this was the scene at Hugo's for Hair. I walk into the shop and there's Hugo, dancing behind this customer. He's about thirty, kind of pudgy, in baggy surfer shorts, bright shirt. He looks like Pedro Almodóvar. And he's dancing to that Madonna song, "Wrap Me Up In Your Love." Remember that song? Very infectious, euphoric. The only thing she ever did that I categorically liked.

But as soon as he sees me he stops, he stops dancing, gets this freaked look. Of course, I'm not wearing dark glasses, so my eyes must look crazy. I'm sweaty and tweaked.

So I tell him who I am, and he says, "Yes, I know. Reese told me about you." He has a thick accent.

He gets this other operator to take over for him, and he leads me through the back to his apartment. Which is stuffed with female-identified Hollywood movie kitsch. Like Joan Crawford posters, Lana Turner stills, *All About Eve*, that kind of stuff. His sister is in the kitchen, cooking and watching a small TV. Hugo doesn't introduce us. I get the feeling she's very shy.

So I start to ask him about Reese, telling him I just heard about Reese's death. And I'm trying to present myself as somewhat open-minded about all this mumbo-jumbo shit. But what I'm really looking for is something I can use against Pablo. I don't believe this shit, that's *my* protection. But Pablo believes it, so maybe there's some way I can turn it against him. That's what I'm looking for.

But I've barely started fishing when Hugo says, "You're in grave danger. This man [Pablo] is a *padero* [a Palo Mayombe priest]. He has raped your soul. You are going to die unless you submit to exorcism."

I feel like saying: Right. How much is that going to cost? How much did Reese pay you? Instead I just say, "That doesn't seem to have worked too well with Reese."

He says, "My magic was not powerful enough. I did not know then what I know now. This *padero* has killed."

I ask him what he means.

"He has killed a young man," Hugo says. "He has made of him a human sacrifice to the vile gods of Palo Mayombe. You see, your friend [Reese] was free for a time. I dispelled the curse placed upon him by the killing of his cat. There is only one way he could be driven to his suicidal act. This *padero*, he has taken the life of an innocent young man."

At this point I ask to use the bathroom. I have to take a leak, but mostly I'm feeling this strange sense of panic. Like an anxiety attack. In the bathroom I splash water on my face. But I'm suddenly feeling this incredible physical exhaustion, like the speed has completely dehydrated me and sapped my batteries. So I do some more. I snort two fat lines off the counter. Which revives me. Except that when I step back out I feel like I'm in some other dimension. I'm almost giddy in this strange way, and everything looks glazed.

"You're speeding," Hugo says.

"Yeah, so what?" I say.

"No, it's good," he says. "It will help you to do what you must do."

So we're standing there by the kitchen, and I'm pouring sweat from the speed, and Hugo starts telling me about this exorcism or whatever it is he wants to perform tomorrow at noon. Like it has to happen at noon for some reason. And I'm standing there listening but my mind is going in and out of what he's saying. And his accent is irritating. I have to ask him to repeat things. Like he says, "It's gray." And I say, "What's gray?"

And he says, his magic. Like normally he's just into white magic. But Pablo's magic is so black, Hugo has to appropriate certain black techniques in order to fight it. That's what he's trying to tell me. It's this theoretical discussion of magic.

I finally say, "Look, this is interesting. But what if I just kill Pablo? How's that?"

He says, "No, no. That wouldn't save you. His curse would still be in place."

This pisses me off. It's just not something I want to hear. I'm not completely immune to superstition.

This is where I notice the TV in the kitchen. I'm kind of staring at it idly, this small black-and-white TV, showing a movie in Spanish. And it's just as I'm realizing what the film is—that it's Warren Oates in *Alfredo Garcia*, dubbed in Spanish—that Hugo says, "It's in his brain. It's the only way. Like that. Do you see what I am saying?"

So believe it, Jim, I reel. Since I see what he's up to. Like he doesn't want to say it in so many words. But he's telling me I've got to cut off Pablo's head.

I'm not imagining this, incidentally. When I look at Hugo, he's looking at the TV, where Warren Oates is stuffing the severed head into a burlap sack. And he says, "Do you see?"

I say, "Yeah, I get the picture. But I gotta tell you, man, you are even crazier than I am."

Except here's the thing. Here's the thing right now. I'm not sure that he is. He might be, but I'm not sure of it. Because the truth is, it was one of those moments. One of those epiphanies that you really can't ignore. Since *Bring Me the Head of Alfredo Garcia* is a major film, a major reference, in *Testosterone*. You know how I feel about that film. How I've always had this major thing about that film. Long before I ever met Pablo. I love that film. It's this major sick classic. So of course I was using it in *Testosterone*.

But what are the chances that film would be on TV just at that point? Just when Hugo needed it to indicate to me what I need to do? What are the chances of that? Tell me that's a fluke.

So you see what I'm saying. Something like that is very hard to ignore. Even if you don't believe in magic.

So what I'm thinking is this. I'm glad you're not here. That you can't stop me. And I'm trying not to even think of what you'd say. Because it's like this. I think I'd like to be prepared. Just in case I want to do it. In case I decide it's the way to go. I can't cut off his head with a baseball bat or a gun.

This is strange. It's not like I haven't thought of it before. Cutting off his head. I've thought of it a lot. As an image. A satisfying image. But it's messy. Inevitably. Which itself might be satisfying. In real life, I mean. It might be very satisfying. I might just want to do it. To have the option of doing it. Decide about the other shit later. Once I've got his head in a sack.

The more I think about it, the more I like it. It makes a lot of sense in a lot of different ways. Plus, it feels inevitable. All these thoughts and fantasies culminating in the deed itself.

I've always felt that fantasies are powerful. Be careful what you dream about, because you may pull it into your life. So maybe if I'd thought about New Mexico more.... But that's like dreaming of Mengele in paradise. I can't save Pablo. I'm not Jesus. I'm not a magician. I'm just a fag with a gun who needs a chainsaw. And here's a Builder's Emporium coming up on the left.

* * *

OK, that was fun. Man, I got some looks. My eyes, I guess. I don't care. But I didn't like the chainsaws. I checked out a few. I like the *idea* of a chainsaw. The idea of *that sound*. If I had him tied up and I cranked up a chainsaw, you *know* he would shit, probably literally. I like the idea of him shitting. I don't mean in a scat sense. But I like the idea of Pablo that scared. You know what *that sound* does, because of all the movies. So you know he would shit if I was playing Leatherface.

But that noise has a downside. Since I don't know where I'm going to do this yet. There's no way to know yet. But I might not want the racket. I might not want to find a place so isolated that no one else would hear the chainsaw.

So I got a machete instead. I'm looking at it now. It's nice and new and sharp. Warren Oates used a machete. It's quiet. And in some ways more satisfying. More visceral. More *hands-on*, in a way. A chainsaw is really too effortless. Like carving a roast with an electric knife. I don't want this to be too easy. I want to really get off on this. Get my anger out, *express it*. So this is much better, I think.

They didn't have handcuffs. I didn't ask, but I thought about it and decided they wouldn't. I couldn't see where they'd come into the home improvement picture. Unless you wanted to handcuff and butt-fuck Bob Vila. Which is not something I'd want to do.

So I got some three-inch duct tape to use inside of handcuffs. I can also use it to tape his mouth. Just regular duct tape, the silver stuff.

Then I thought about trash bags, but that's no good. For one thing, the shape would show. I can't see walking around with a head in a trash bag. The obvious shape of a nose. Not that I plan to take a stroll down Whittier Boulevard. Or any other boulevard. But you never know what might happen.

Mostly, though, I don't want it to rot or start to decay. Hugo didn't mention this, but I know it's a factor. That's what's going on. He's making a *nganga*. And it's no good, it doesn't work, if the brain isn't fresh. The brain you put into the *nganga*. I'm not sure how gray this magic is.

So I've got a Sidekick. A Rubbermaid Sidekick. That's the cute name of this nice little ice chest. All I need now is ice. So I don't end up like Warren Oates with the flies buzzing in the car.

Maybe I'm crazy. I don't know. I don't care anymore.

❈   ❈   ❈

OK, I'm in Hollywood now. Deep Hollywood. Parked in the lot of a scumbag 7-Eleven. I'm sitting in the land of fifty thousand losers, and I've got the ice now. And a gay rag. A *Frontiers*. It's almost six-thirty. I'm still killing time.

Looking at the personals. Which isn't totally idle. According to Reese, Pablo's into the personals. Looking for masochists, conscious or otherwise. When he needs a quick vampire fix.

Here's a fun ad. For an HIV-positive orgy. It says, "Mild KS lesions OK." What's mild? Who decides? Does someone at the door count them? "I'm sorry. It's ten lesions or less." Also, "No herpes or TB." Well, that's cool. I can understand that. It says, "Safe sex." And in parentheses, "Sucking cock, fucking with condoms." Hmm. OK, I'm not going to bring up precome and preshoot and drizzle. I'm not going to spoil the party. Since it looks like I'm invited too. It says, "HIV-adjusted also welcome." That's me. If I don't find Pablo, I can always suck some cock with the mild lesion crowd. It's good to have a fallback plan.

Wait a second. Hmm. OK, this is interesting. It's an ad for a sex club. Which, it appears, has special hours on weekends. An early bird special, you could say. Which surprises me, actually. I wasn't really planning to go there till much later, but...I think I'm going to drive by now and see what I can see.

✣ ✣ ✣

On Santa Monica Boulevard now. The hustler area near La Brea. These guys. Look at this guy here. Schlong down his pants leg, white tank top, greasy Elvis hair. Classic.

I'm so naive about hustlers. I mean, the few times I've

thought about it is when I've really wanted a blow job. But I've never been sure if you pay them to suck you off or if it's the other way around. Like you'd get one of these guys in your car and he'd say, "Oh, no, man. You pay me fifty bucks to blow me." Which is not really something I'd be into.

I heard some story once about a guy stopping to pick up a hustler. Some guy, a husband, with a baby seat in his car. "Hi, honey. Had to work late."

I mean, you have to assume that most of these guys have it.

OK, here's my turn. OK, let me check the addresses. It's along here somewhere. It's all businesses along here. Light industrial places. Thirty-three, thirty-five. OK, that's it.

Hmm. OK. I'm idling here. Checking it out. Here comes someone now. Along the sidewalk. Black guy. Arsenio Hall look. How dated. Hey, for all I know, it *is* Arsenio. I can see it on *Hard Copy*. Arsenio's Secret Shame. Since his show was canceled, etcetera, blah, blah. Arsenio's Downward Spiral. I'll bet he's going to get his rocks off. He's almost at the address. Will he turn? Yes. There he goes.

OK, there's a parking lot. Which is full. So I was right. A lot of guys are into the early bird special.

OK, I'm backing up a little, so I can check out the cars. I'm no longer looking for a Saab, incidentally. According to Stan, Reese found out that Pablo's driving a pickup now. A full-sized Ford or Chevy. And wouldn't you know, there's one in the lot. It looks like a Chevy, a black Chevy pickup, new, so it could be him. For what it's worth, though, I'm not feeling anything. It's just a truck. I'm not getting any gut-grabbing flash of intuition. One downside to speed: My mind's moving too fast to get a fix on anything. But that could be his truck. He could be inside. So I'd better organize myself with a plan.

I had a feeling he'd gotten rid of the Saab. It was too yuppie, too eighties. I'll bet he's gone queer clone by now, too. Or postqueer clone. With an Auschwitz buzz cut. Wait and see if I'm not right.

OK, I'm going to park out here on the street. Don't want to get blocked in by some sex addict's Samurai.

Man, I'm jacked up now. Almost too jacked up. My heart's really pounding, Jim. Speed and adrenaline are a killing mix.

I'm taking the Glock. That's what I've got. A Glock nine-millimeter. Gangbanger special. *Glock.* Cool name. Rhymes with *cock*. I'd like to make him suck my Glock, but I guess that's out now. I'm going to shove it down my butt crack, under my waistband. My T-shirt should hide it. I just don't think they'd let me in with a machete. Maybe they would. If I did some fast talking. I almost feel like I could. I almost feel that omnipotent. That I could convince them it was just a weird prop. Like I have a cane-cutter fetish or something. I almost think that. That I could convince anyone of anything.

But I'm not that foolish. I'm not quite that euphoric. So I'll just take the Glock. I think if he's there, once he sees the gun, he'll do what I tell him. Or if I see him, I can leave and wait until he comes out. It's getting dark now. That's the best plan actually. Stick the Glock in his back in the parking lot.

It was easier before, though. The way I pictured it before. That if I found him in the sex club, I could do it right there. Tap him on the shoulder while he's in a group scene. As soon as our eyes meet, shoot him in the forehead. Or stuff the gun into his mouth.

This is more complicated. I'll be back.

❋ ❋ ❋

OK, I'm out of here. Oh, man, I think I blew it. Let me get out of here. Fuck. I don't think they'd dare call the cops though. I'm probably OK.

Hold on. Let me make sure I'm getting out of here. What the fuck street is this? Romaine? What's this up here? It must be Highland. Fuck. OK, I'm running the light. Fuck it.

That wasn't smart. But I guess I'm OK. Shit, I've still got a hard-on. I think I'm insane.

Man, I'm still shaken. I really thought it was him. That poor guy. I think I scared the fuck out of him.

So, OK. So I go in the door and there's a window. I have to show ID and all that, which is fucked. Because of course they've got my name now. But I really can't see them calling the cops. They've already been hassled. I mean, these sex club places are kind of controversial. Even though they've sprung up all over now. And gotten progressively bolder in their gay-rag ads. Instead of being the guilty secret they were a few years ago. Now they're almost proudly proclaiming: *Yes, we spread HIV through multi-partner cock sucking and unprotected butt fucking. Won't you please come join us on our fabulous death boat, the SS Jonestown. Special college boy discount rates. Just show us your fresh uninfected buns and student ID.*

Of course, if you say anything, if you point out that these places are mass-suicide parlors, they call you sex-negative.

Which no self-respecting PC queer wants to be. And the Health Department, the liberal supervisors who are all taking fag money—nobody gives a shit or does anything. They're probably thinking: Fuck, we give up. If those fags want to kill themselves, why should we try to stop them? And you know what? They've got a point.

Anyway, I show the guy at the window my license. And I can see him noting the birth date, then checking me out, making this judgment call. That OK, I may be thirty-eight, but I don't look *that* old. Or I won't under a twenty-watt red light bulb. Because it turns out that most of the guys inside are young. In their twenties. The new sex-positive seroconversion set.

So I get my card, all that, he buzzes me in. It's very dark, of course. My geriatric eyes need time to adjust. So the first thing I notice is the music and the smell. The music is that U2 song, "One." Which I really like, but it's a strange, moody, grief-riddled, heavily AIDS-coded song, which seems like a very bleak comment on this scene. Like this incredibly moving, rehumanizing, deobjectifying *comment*. But I get the feeling I'm the only one who's taking it that way.

It's this labyrinthine place. Guys wandering around through the plywood cubicles and corridors. Glory holes everywhere. Smell of piss and stale come. Some guy back in one urine-scented booth, hunched in the shadows, squatting on a toilet that doesn't work. He's emaciated, like he's got maybe three T-cells left, and he sticks out his tongue. I don't think he wants to blow me. I think he wants me to piss in his mouth. Last call.

Another guy, with a honey-blond beard, is kind of listlessly jerking off in a barred, jail-like cubicle. Like Vincent van Gogh on crystal. So fried, he's kind of talking to himself. Like muttering sex talk to himself. He worries me. Like I half-expect him to flash a straight razor or something. Cut off his ear. Or his dick or something. He looks just like Kirk Douglas in *Lust for Life*. Except the more fitting title is *Lust for Death*.

The whole place reminds me of the old Basic Plumbing. Which got to be so mean, I quit going there way before AIDS, just because of the attitudes, the evil, callous way guys treated each other. So I'm having all these flashbacks about things I haven't seen or felt since 1981.

I mean, it's crowded but nobody's really doing that much. Just walking around, like bored rats in a maze. Like the bigger the selection, the pickier people get. So there's this air of frustration. This sense of judgment, of tense restraint. It doesn't seem very warmhearted. That's the term that *L.A Weekly* moron used in his PC propaganda piece a while back. "Unlike the sex clubs of yesteryear, the new sexual anarchy is warmhearted...." Something like that. Maybe I'm missing something, but it seems about as joyful as Buchenwald.

I see one guy with a goatee, which makes me quake for a second. Till I notice the hair on his forearms, which Pablo doesn't have. So I make the rounds a few times, feel a few looks of interest, which is cheaply reassuring. I finally see some action. Three or four guys around another guy, who's down on his knees. But it feels disembodied for some reason. Like the first time I ever went to a bathhouse, in the seventies. Even though there were other times, later, when the same scene, say...at the beach, might have turned me on. Like I'd get a hard-on and join the crowd. But this doesn't thrill me. It's like looking at a porno photo that no longer turns you on.

Speaking of porno, that's my next stop. The room that's like a lounge with a TV monitor showing a tape. But I don't stay there long. This tape's completely insane. It's like four of five guys in this intense, frenetic scene. Like this rough sex scene where they're yelling abuse: "Suck his cock, you cock-hungry pig." But that's not what bothers me. It's the pitch the film's maintaining. The frantic, borderline hysteria. Like some abject fiend on the edge of coming. Except it never stops. There's just this sense of frantic violence that goes on and on. And the sound's also fucked up for some reason, distorting. So you hear these garbled yells of: "Suck on it! Choke on it, choke on it, you pig!" And it seems very clear that sex is not enough, that they'd don't want to fuck, they want to fucking kill each other. So you're starting to feel: Why don't they just cut the shit and *do it*! Forget about their dicks, whip out a goddamn machete. Let's see some fucking *blood*! That's what you *want*!

So I have to get out of there. I feel like this tape is ridiculing me. Turning what I feel, what for me is very serious, into a cheap porno conceit. As if the culture, the gay consumerist culture, wants to defuse and neutralize me.

So I kind of stumble down the corridor, feeling panicked, even paranoid. Like everyone sees me as some floridly short-circuiting pathetic loser who isn't cold enough to function in this scene. Like I should be stuck in the dumpster out back like a broken, discarded replicant. So I duck into one of the cubicles, just to get away from all the eyes.

It's like a stall with a door on a spring. So I hook the door and try to collect myself. And I can smell marijuana smoke in the air, which I've smelled since I came in, and that reminds me of the joint I lifted at Reese's. Guess I haven't mentioned that until now. Not especially proud of it. But there was a box, a cigar box on the coffee table, filled with maybe two dozen joints. Didn't think Reese would miss one. I thought it might help bring me down from the speed, when I needed to do that. I stuck it in my pocket a second before Stan came in.

Now feels like the time to bring myself down some, so I fire up the joint in the cubicle. And it's odd. This other strange song starts to play. I mean, strange for the setting. That Frente! acoustic version of "Bizarre Love Triangle," which is one of my two favorite New Order songs. I mean, it was weird the first time I heard the Frente! version, since I've been singing that song to myself for years. My own acoustic version in the car, in the shower, idly walking around the house. I like the chorus especially, [sings] where you get down on your knees and pray...

Which is maybe what I should be doing now. Praying. If I knew who to pray to or what to pray for, but I don't anymore.

And so for a while I was gone. I mean, the dope was good, very good, and for a while I was lost in the sad lost world of that song. Like I could write a whole novel, a Proustian novel, about everything that went through my mind in those three minutes.

But then the song was over and there was nothing for a moment. And that's when I heard these two guys talking in the next cubicle. Like having this conversation after sex. And I reel because this one guy is saying, "So my friend John goes: 'I don't know why you keep attracting these guys who always get obsessed with you.' And I go, 'John, it's because I have a kind of sexual magnetism that I can't turn off—'"

So it's him. It has to be him. It's his voice, his phrasing, it's him.

Except I'm buzzed now, from the dope, so how can I be sure my mind isn't playing tricks? That's when I notice the peephole. I turn down the light in my cubicle and crouch down and look through the peephole. Meanwhile the other guy's talking, all very low-key, about his boring job as a claims adjuster or something. So I look through the peep hole, and there they are on a small cot. I can't see a lot at first in the weak yellow light. Their crotches mostly. They've taken their clothes off. You can see their limp dicks, their hands holding cigarettes, as they go on talking. But I'm sure it's him.

"I'm working on this paper now. It's really been exhausting me," he says. Playing grad student on study break.

Then he reaches over to stub out his cigarette and I see his moustache and goatee. I see his Auschwitz buzz cut, as predicted. So I have no further doubt that it's him.

Then the other guy gets up, pulls on his pants, says he has to take a leak.

Pablo says, "So you're going back on Tuesday?" Like the guy's from out of town. Like Pablo wants to spend some more time with him. So I know I have to act now, before the guy comes back and they can leave together.

I don't have time to think, or to savor the anticipation. Which is somewhat disappointing, that the moment is coming so fast. I take out the Glock, hold it under my T-shirt as I step out. I press the door to his cubicle. It's unlatched. I enter, pulling out the gun. He jumps as I say, "Don't make a fucking sound."

That's when I see all the hair on his chest and stomach and know it's not Pablo. I still don't want to believe it, though. I was so sure. I keep looking at his face, as though his body could be lying. Like he's grown hair on his chest to fool me, to fuck with my head. Which is crazy, I know. But my mind really wants to be right.

Finally I have to admit it though. It's not his face either. This guy's nose is too long, his cheeks too sunken. So I say, "Look, sorry. I thought you were someone else."

So that's when I leave. And then this strange thing happens. Except it's not so strange, which is why I'm very concerned now. But as I step outside, into the bracing night air, I suddenly get an erection. Like for no apparent reason. Except I think at first it's maybe some weird form of relief. Like I've been in this hellhole of death, this stinking, suffocating prison, and now I'm busting free, embracing the fresh night air and life or something. I don't want to admit yet what's really going on. It's too horrendous.

But I'm admitting it now. Because I've still got a hard-on. It's been a half hour now and it still hasn't gone down. I can't wait any longer. The stakes are too high. It's the hemp that did it. My doctor warned me about that. That it can cause this kind of side effect. Smoking dope when you're taking Desyrel. I thought about it at Reese's when I lifted the joint. I guess I just didn't believe it. Or maybe I was thinking, when I smoked it in the sex club, maybe I was thinking, if I'm really honest, that as foul as the place was, if I got a killer hard-on, I might just have gotten all this sucked out of my system.

But I'm in trouble now. I'm in deep shit, I can tell. It's a different kind of hard-on. I mean, it's a great hard-on. Like an *extra-hard* hard-on. But the problem is this. I'm not thinking about sex. And I can tell I could think about anything—Pat Boone, Rush Limbaugh naked, Nancy Reagan's twat—*and I would not lose this erection.*

Which may sound funny. Or like a highly desirable state. Boy, you could fuck all night, ha ha. But here's the thing. If I don't do something now, this could permanently damage me. Make me permanently impotent. Which is really no joke at all. That's why I'm closing in on Cedars [Sinai Hospital] right now.

※ ※ ※

OK, I'm back. It's about eleven. A lot's been going on. I'm moving, as you can tell. I feel OK now. Leveled out. Just did some more speed. I kind of had to. They hit me up with something at Cedars. Valium or something. They could tell I was tweaked. But right now I feel perfect. Wired but not frantic. In control.

Which is good. I feel like this is it. I'm closing in. It's going to happen. I've never been more sure of anything in my life.

So I go into Emergency. Which for starters is painfully bright. And I've got my T-shirt out and all that. But it's not completely covering my crotch. So I'm very self-conscious. Like some teenage kid with a boner who has to share in front of the class.

The waiting room's not crowded, fortunately. Just this elderly Jewish couple. I kind of walk to the Admissions window half turned away from them. The guy at the window turns out to be the problem. This icky young queen who reminds me of Calvin. Calvin pre-AIDS. So he asks me what the problem is, and I tell him I've got an erection.

He says, "We should all be so lucky."

And I say, "No, look, this isn't a joke. I'm taking Desyrel, this antidepressant, and this is one of the side effects. It gives you this permanent erection, and if you don't do something about it, it can physically damage your penis."

I realize this old Jewish couple can hear me. And this queen is kind of smiling. And I'm starting to feel like no one's going to believe me. Like no one here is going to know what I'm talking about.

"How long have you had it?" the guy asks.

"I don't know. Forty-five minutes."

"You mean, constantly?"

"Yes."

He's looking at me like he thinks I'm a nutcase. Or like if the Jewish couple weren't there in the waiting room, he'd ask me to show him.

I say, "Look, this is serious. I need to see a doctor immediately."

So he finally takes my Blue Cross card and all that. Then he says, "Why don't you have a seat, Mr. Seagrave? It'll be a few minutes."

So I say, "Look, man. You're not getting it. I know this sounds silly or something, compared to gunshot victims and people having heart attacks. But it's a very real thing! If I'm not treated, damage will result. I'll be impotent, man! Don't you get it? Maybe you don't give a shit, but it's my fucking life! I want to see a doctor, and I want to see him now!"

So he goes and talks to someone, and this nurse comes and gets me. She leads me back into one of the examining places, and I have to tell her all over again what's going on. Then finally the doctor comes in, this young Jewish guy who I recognize immediately from a local news show. Like he's this doctor who always does the medical reports. So I explain for a third time what's going on, and he wants to see. But this nurse is still there, and I know she's a nurse, but I say, "Do you think she could step out? I'm shy, OK?"

So she does, and I show the doctor my boner, which is totally huge and dark red. I mean, the color freaks me out, it's so dark, like all the blood in my dick is clotting or something.

And the doctor says, "Are you sure you weren't just stimulated?"

And I almost say, No, I was just at this truly vile sex club that if anything had the opposite effect. But I decide not to mention that, in case he's homophobic or something. But I'm already getting terrified, since I can tell he doesn't know anything about this. He's got this expression like he's thinking: This is a puzzler.

I say, "Look, I knew this could happen. If you smoke marijuana. My doctor gave me that warning. I just didn't take it that seriously. But I know there are drugs you can give me that will counteract the effect."

I didn't want to say anything more. Because I knew, I remembered this conversation with my doctor that seemed like a joke at the time, that if the drugs didn't work they had to do surgery. Cut the blood vessels or something. Which will also result in impotence. That's part of why I don't want this guy to know I'm gay. He might say, "Sorry, Bud. Only one way to deal with *this*."

But this guy just looks baffled. Then he goes and uses the phone. Which seems to take forever. Getting through to some other doctor. I can see him from the examining room. At one point he laughs into the phone. And I'm thinking: Man, chat it up some other time, dude. This is fucking *serious,* you asshole!

Finally he comes and gives me a shot of something. As he does it, he says, "If this doesn't work, we may have to perform surgery. Which could leave you impotent."

I say, "Oh, man. My girlfriend will shit." Not taking any chances, since I'm kind of at his mercy.

Then he says, "Your pupils are dilated. What else have you taken tonight?"

So I tell him I did a couple lines of crank, since I was working on a project. That's when he calls for the Valium shot.

Then it's like this waiting game. This big suspense scene. Like if it's going to work, it should work within minutes. So the doctor's there, and so is the nurse. And other people are kind of watching from farther back. Like everyone in the ER knows what's going on.

I'm just sitting on the table at this point. My pants are up, my shirt's covering my crotch, so everybody's watching my face, like I'm supposed to tell them if there's any change.

I'm really thinking if this doesn't work, I'm going to kill myself. Since I can't see living if I can't fuck.

The tension gets unbelievable. Not that I care a lot, since I'm kind of peaking on Valium. But on another level, I still know what's at stake. The doctor keeps looking at his watch. I half expect him to say at any moment, "We tried. Call surgery."

But finally I say, "OK, I feel something. It's going down. Yeah, it is."

The doctor wants to see it again, so I make him draw the curtain. Like I don't need an audience watching me lose my erection.

And it's OK. It's going down. Way down. Until my dick's so

shriveled up it looks like it was dipped in ice water. At which point I get panicked. I say, "Look, this isn't permanent—"

He says, "No, no. You'll be fine in a day or two. But you should definitely avoid restimulation."

*R*estimulation? Like he still thinks I was probably fucking.

Anyway, that was it. They wanted me to stay there and rest for an hour or so, just to be sure. They didn't try to have me admitted, like I thought they might.

But I left after about forty minutes, because I got this idea about checking upstairs.

There's this big AA meeting there at Cedars on Saturday nights that I went to once with Phil years ago. And I suddenly remembered that Mark had said he'd met Pablo there. That's where they met. And with this new knowledge that Reese had also been in AA at one time, I wondered if maybe one of Pablo's specialties is preying on fragile, recovering alcoholics. It was worth a look anyway, as long as I was already there.

So the meeting is already under way. This fat woman—I mean large, full-figured, hefty, whatever the correct term is. This gargantuan fag hag speaker's at the podium, doing shtick. You know how AA is. Like she'll say, "And then I fell down in my own puke." And everybody guffaws. Which is OK. I'm not putting AA down. It's saved a lot of lives.

It's an oppressive crowd, though. Very West Hollywood, people dressed for effect in this strident, desperate, cutting-edge fashion way. Lots of good-looking guys, though, I have to admit. A few too many icky-perfect muscle queens. But here and there an intelligent, bohemian knockout. Also, Sappho City. k.d. lang types. Packs of Jodie Foster look-alikes.

So I'm scanning this crowd of a hundred or so, looking for a goatee. Even though I know Pablo may not have one anymore. And it's frustrating, since I'm not wearing my glasses. I notice several goatees, but I can't really make out the faces that well.

Then I feel a tap on my shoulder. It's Mark. He seems cordial until he sees my eyes or something. Then he says, "My God, are you all right?"

So I decide not to bullshit him, there's no point. I just say, "Yeah, I'm fine. Is he here?"

So Mark says, "Oh, God. I was afraid of this."

So he leads me outside to this balcony where we can talk. He says, "Listen to me. You're insane right now, I can see it. I feel responsible. I should never have told you about the animals."

I say, "Look, it's not just animals he's killing."

Mark says, "I know. He's killing you right now. You're going to end up like Reese."

I say, "You don't understand. I'm not going to end up like Reese. Like Reese or like you. Reese is dead and you're dying. I'm not going to end up like either of you."

That kind of stops him. Since it's harsh but true. I just leave it at that. No way am I going to try to explain about cutting off Pablo's head. Try to get his approval for something like that. I like Mark but he's too much of a wuss, into all this therapy-talk, think-positive shit. He's one of these people who will *talk* about their anger, and *understand* yours. But when it comes to *action*, even when it could save his life, he's a typical homo victim. *We are a gentle people.*

So I just say, "Look, I'll see you around."

As I start down the steps, he says, "You're destroying yourself."

"Thanks for being supportive," I tell him without looking back.

OK, I'm almost there. I'm coming to Sunset Boulevard. This is the best bet of any all day. Because I'll tell you what happened. After I left Mark I stopped at a liquor store to snag some more Evian, and while I was there, I picked up an *L.A. Weekly*. It's a credit to me that I wasn't in despair at this point. Since I had no more concrete ideas, other than to check out a few bars and one other sex club. But I was not in despair. I still had this feeling that I was somehow on track. And then I opened the *Weekly* and bam, there it was. The Jesus and Mary Chain at the Palladium, one night only.

If Pablo's still alive and in this city, he'll be there.

※ ※ ※

OK, I'm parked on Sunset across from the Palladium. The show's still going on. Once people start coming out, I'm going to pull up by the entrance. I can't see shit from here without my glasses.

It's after midnight. I don't know how long these guys play. But I know he's going to be here. I know it. There was some X show a while back. Some benefit show. I remember thinking when I saw the ad: He won't miss that. And I'll bet he didn't. But that was during the "compassionate" period.

It's strange. Back at the liquor store, I saw the book Reese gave me about the Matamoros killings. *Buried Secrets*. It's out in paperback now, and they've got Adolfo Constanzo's photo on the cover. Like they know he's hot. He *is* attractive, appealing, just visually. Eye-catching. Like people will impulse-buy the paperback without knowing what a vile monster this handsome guy is. How he tied up this blond kid and fucked him in the ass. Then cut out his heart and split his skull open like a coconut. Scooped out his gringo med student brain. And that's just one scene. One of many. It was the one time he did an Anglo though. A white blond American. That was his big, irresistible mistake.

Oh, wow. I'm just remembering something. Something Pablo said once. When we were in bed. This was early on. For some reason we got into this thing about Mexico. About *Old Gringo*. I think that was it. I think that's how it started. Since Pablo liked Carlos Fuentes. But he thought the film sucked. The film with Jane Fonda and Gregory Peck. I hadn't seen it, but I told him I'd heard that it sucked. Then we talked about Ambrose Bierce and *Bring Me the Head of Alfredo Garcia*. And *Under the Volcano*. How these Anglos go to Mexico looking for redemption but instead find alcoholic madness and death. And Pablo said something about it not just being Anglos. That a friend of his was killed down there in a shoot-out with police. "He got involved with drugs," Pablo said. "Which was really stupid."

He said a friend, not a boyfriend. But of course he wouldn't want to tell me too much or present it in a way that would make me ask more questions.

That's how Constanzo died. In a shoot-out with police in Mexico City. Actually, he killed himself. He and his macho boyfriend. They shot themselves in a closet as the cops were closing in.

Adolfo had two boyfriends. This macho guy, Martin

[Rodriguez]. A fem guy, Omar [Ochoa]. Omar got captured but later died of AIDS. So probably the whole gang had AIDS, since they were all fucking each other.

Which makes me wonder about Pablo. If he was fucking Adolfo in '87.

According to Reese, Pablo feels protected. That his magic protects from arrest, from getting AIDS. Which raises some interesting questions in a way. Not that I think he *is* protected. But if he *believes* he is, does that in fact provide protection? Because belief is very important. That's why I wouldn't take the HIV test for a long time. Because it seemed like voodoo. A positive test result would be like a voodoo curse. A self-fulfilling prophecy.

But I don't know about all this *belief* shit. I mean, all these people who try to think good thoughts. That Louise Hay/Marianne Williamson stuff. Where they insist on saying that AIDS is not a fatal disease. Just "life-challenging." Except it's kind of crossed a line now. From "life-challenging" to "life-enhancing." I mean: "AIDS is a gift. A beautiful experience." Testing positive's "like the moment where it goes from black-and-white to color in *The Wizard of Oz*." Some moron actually wrote that in one of the local gay rags. "I feel keenly alive now." Gee, sounds good. Better than acid. Think I'll go out and get infected. Guess you're not really living unless you're also dying. Being HIV-negative is so drab and gray, like a washed-out sixteen-millimeter film noir print. I want to see the world in Metrocolor, too!

The Believers. That was the Matamoros gang's favorite film. They had a cassette of it. Watched it all the time. It's not very good. It's pretty hokey. John Schlesinger directed it.

James Robert Baker

Came out in '87. The best scene is up front. Where Martin Sheen's wife gets electrocuted by a Mr. Coffee. It's shorting out, and she touches it while standing barefoot in spilled milk. Martin Sheen watches from the doorway, howling, "Oh, God! Oh, God!" for what seems like at least a full minute while his wife stands there crackling and frying. After that, it's all downhill. A lot of fake Santeria shit and some plot involving WASP businessmen sacrificing their own sons so they can stay in the Fortune 500 or something. But I can see why Adolfo liked it. He probably did a freeze-frame on the shots of dead boys with their hearts torn out and jacked off.

OK. All right. People are coming out. Yeah, this is it. It's over. OK, I've got to get over there.

Fuck. I'm trying to make a U-turn, but it's not going to happen. I don't believe this traffic. Shit, they're flooding out now, too. I've got to get over there. This is fucked up. OK, fuck it. I'm going up to the light.

Come on, you fucker, change. Shit, people are flooding out. It's a mob scene and I'm stuck here. Behind some fuck who's playing with his dick. Come on, man. Do it! Make your fucking turn! [hits the horn] Shit, the light's changing. You fuckhead! Goddamn you, you fuck!

OK, OK. Let's take it down a notch. It's my turn next. Oh, man. Look at this. Here comes a mob in the crosswalk. Oh, man. I know he's here. If I'm this close and I miss him....

Oh, fuck. Oh, shit. It's him. Jim, I'm not kidding. It's him, I swear. Here he comes. He's in the crosswalk. He's with some other guy. Oh, shit. I wish I weren't here. I feel like Janet Leigh in *Psycho* with her boss in the crosswalk. If he looks over and sees me, I'm dead. Here he comes. Oh, Jesus. It's *him*! He's still got his fucking goatee. And an Auschwitz buzz cut, what did I tell you. *It's him.* Here he comes. He's right in front of the car. Don't look over. God, please stop him from looking over. Right, just keep walking. Talk to your friend, that's right. That's right.

Shit, man. It's him. I've found my man.

OK, they're walking down the street. To that side street. What is it? El Centro. They must be parked nearby. I've got to get over there. If I lose him now, I'll kill myself. Time to get radical. Look out, you fucks. Here I come. Hit your brakes, fuckers. You don't know who you're fucking with. Just get the fuck out of my way.

OK, I'm over. Let's turn down here. I've got to get back over there. Over to El Centro. I can't afford to miss them. What was the other guy wearing? Light pants. Beige Dockers or something. So let's look for a guy in light pants.

OK, here's El Centro. Is that them? Yes.

Right. And there's the truck. The pickup. It's a full-size Ford. Pablo's unlocking the passenger door. How polite.

OK. What are they doing? Are they go to sit there and jack off? No. He's starting the engine. The lights. He's backing up now.

OK, this is it. This is it, man! I'm elated, believe it. What did I tell you? Did I tell you I'd find him? I knew it. I never stopped believing it would happen.

OK. I'm following them down El Centro now. I should stay farther back, but I don't want to lose him. The traffic's pretty heavy, though. And I'm just headlights. Even if he sees this car, it won't mean anything to him. If he'd looked over in the crosswalk, I'd be dead, though. Thank God he didn't. He was talking to his friend.

I don't know what to make of the other guy. Glasses, receding hair. Professorial. A new, trusting victim.

OK, he's turning on Melrose. Turning west. Man, I am jacked up.

Oh, man. I don't like this. This stretch of Melrose. It's too bright. I've got to stay back. If I get caught right behind them at a red light, he might make me in the rearview mirror. He could. It's that bright.

So I'm getting farther back. Changing lanes. OK.

It's late. It's twelve-thirty. They must be going home. Either to Pablo's or the other guy's place. I'll bet this is some kind of date. That's the word the other guy would use. He looks like a guy who'd *date*.

Or maybe they're living together. Who knows? Pablo could be using this guy. Using his condo as a safe house. You don't know it, buddy, but I'm about to save your life. Your new boyfriend's a serial killer.

"I see you used to have a cat."

"Yes, I did. His name was Gide. He disappeared."

This could involve some waiting, though. A stakeout. I'm glad I've got more crank. Because I really don't want to hurt this other guy. So I may have to wait till Pablo leaves in the morning. If he's spending the night at the other guy's place. Of course, they might go out for breakfast. Breakfast and the beach. This could be a long vigil. Unless they're living together. Then I might be in luck. Because Pablo likes to read the Sunday *New York Times*. I can snag him when he goes out to get it in the morning.

OK, he's getting over to make a left. On...Crescent Heights. Shit, the light's changing. I can't lose them now.

OK, I made it. Going south on Crescent Heights. OK, he's making a right now.

OK. He's making a left on the first street. He's slowing down. OK, he's pulling into a driveway. All right, this is it. I'm going to pull over here.

It's a house. A small Spanish stucco place. They're still sitting in the truck. I can't see what they're doing, it's too dark. The house is dark too, except for the porch light.

OK, they're getting out. They're crossing the lawn. They're stopping. This is odd. It looks like Pablo's inviting him in, but the guy's begging off. They're shaking hands now. *Shaking hands.* Like the other guy's saying, "It was fun, let's keep in touch." Blowing Pablo off. Smart guy.

That's it exactly. The other guy's leaving. Walking out to his car. Pablo's unlocking the front door. He's going in. The other guy's getting into his Mazda.

OK. A light just went on. Back in the house. Like a bedroom light. The front room's still dark.

The other guy's taking off. There he goes.

So. What I'm wondering is this: Does Pablo live here by himself? Or does he have a roommate who might already be asleep?

I think what I'm going to do is take a closer look.

❊   ❊   ❊

OK, I'm on his tail again. There he is. Thank God for the red light. It's changing now. All right, easy, easy. Just keep calm. I don't want to fuck up now.

OK, we're going up Crescent Heights. Shit, I wish there was more traffic. This is getting too obvious. I've got to stay farther back. Which is hard. It's really hard to slow down.

OK, so this is what happened. I sneak up to the house. Along the side of the house. To the back bedroom window. Where I can look in through the bushes and see him.

At first he's undressing, like he's getting ready for bed. It's a weird kind of creepy bedroom. Weird light. Like he's got the overhead light on. Some 1930s fixture with a twenty-watt bulb. So he's pulling off his shirt, his shoes, his black jeans. Then he pulls off his red bikini briefs and he's already got a semierection. He looks at himself in the mirror that's attached to the closet door. His cock kind of jerks as he runs his hand across his pecs. Then he squeezes his cock, transfixed by his own image, like he's about to jack off in the mirror.

Then he stops, like he's considering something. Weighing his options. Does he want to jack off or go out and have sex? I know he's chosen the latter when he pulls on his Levis again. Stuffs his cock down his pants leg.

I duck back farther as he steps to a bureau which is right by the window. He starts looking through T-shirts. He holds up several, including one that says SILENCIO = MUERTE. Then he selects a gray sleeveless model. Which makes me think about the stretch mark on his left biceps. From when he was a fat little homo boy. But I guess he figures that won't show up in the dim light at Cuffs or wherever he's going.

OK, we're on Melrose again, heading east. It's funny. He still looks good. For what that's worth. Which in his case is nothing. But I did have a flash the first second I saw him. When I first looked in the window and saw him undressing. I mean, it triggered some weird memory. Of watching him do the same thing when we were boyfriends. And it would be the same thing. By the time he pulled off his underwear, he'd usually have a semierection. So a part of me still wishes there was some kind of magic that could wipe away everything else and take us back to that. But that's human. To still, even now, have a flash of wistful regret. I don't want to kill the part of myself that can still feel something like that.

Not that I'm getting sentimental. That's part of his curse. He wants you to get so sentimental that you curl up and die and do nothing. That's essentially what happened to Reese. He got sentimental at the sex club and it killed him.

OK, here comes La Brea. What's along here? Didn't that Santa Fe bar used to be along here? Probably something else now. That Santa Fe shit's tired. Except I think we already passed that. There's always Griff's. But that's a new bar now, too, I think. I think it's the Fault Line, coming up on the right. A leather bar for speed freaks. I think that's what it is. That's what their ad says: "We observe the leather ethic." What the fuck is the leather ethic? That you've got to wear black chaps and piss in the mouth of your boyfriend? I don't know. But Pablo's not stopping, so it's a moot point.

It's almost one now. I'll bet he's headed for the hard-core scumbag sector. Silver Lake. I guess the—

TAPE 5

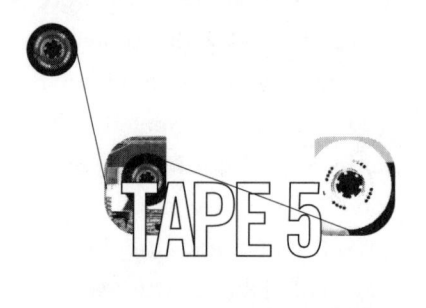

OK, I fucked up. The tape ran out. Around La Brea, I think. Not that you missed much. Just a few random musings. I was right, though. About Silver Lake. That's where I am now. Parked across from the Backfire. He's inside. When he comes out I'm going to nail him.

This is a creepy block. Run-down, dumpy. It looks like a set, almost. A movie set of a dumpy street. An old business section. A Korean market. If that's what it is. Korean, Tibetan. Can't tell from here. Boarded-up storefronts. I don't know what the Backfire used to be. A shoe store, maybe, in 1923.

There's a Laundromat on the corner that's still open even though it's one-twenty now. It must never close. It's creepy too. Like the lights are too dim. Sickly yellow light. Like a brownout's in progress. Or they're trying to save energy. It's similar to Pablo's bedroom. A similar dingy light. Or maybe I'm going blind or something.

Testosterone

Can you hear the music? Maybe not. It's that Nine Inch Nails song. Perfect in a way. That song, "Closer," with the video that has the beating heart. The beating heart that's been cut out and nailed to a board. That nutty Trent Reznor. You know that video? I'll bet it probably won some kind of award. An MTV award. It's that kind of video. It's that insane and startling. Or maybe it's too insane. I don't know.

But it's perfect music for this kind of place. Much more appropriate than "One" or "Bizarre Love Triangle." I'd like to go in. On one level I'm curious. But this place is not like the sex club. It's not all labyrinthine; it's more like a bar with sex going on. He'd see me.

I've been here how long now? Jesus, only ten minutes. It seems like longer. I did some more crank, but I'm crossing a line. Seriously spacing out. An amphetamine zombie. I'm alert but rigid. Like I don't think I've moved a single muscle since I pressed the record button.

But I'm ready to move once he comes out.

This situation is perfect. He parked around the corner on a side street. A very dark side street. And just past his truck there's an alley. That's where I'm going to do it. That's what I've decided. It seems kind of perfect.

It's a good bet he'll be leaving alone. I know where he's at. I know what he's feeling. He's pissed at the guy who blew him off after the concert. He's angry. He's thinking: I'm younger, I'm hotter. Which is true. But he's also Latino. Which he knows some people see as points off. But not all people. So he's looking for someone who wants to suck off a hot young Latino tonight. No muss, no fuss. Cram his fat angry dick through the chain-link fence.

165

That's what he's doing right now, probably. There's a fence inside. That's what guys do. Cram their dicks through it, get worshiped. How do *I* know? I've done it.

I came here one night. About six months ago. When I was "compassionate." I don't know what I was thinking. I tried to tell myself at that point that I wasn't looking for him. But of course I was. And I let a young guy blow me. Through the chain-link fence. A young Latino guy. Who didn't have a goatee, but I imagined he was Pablo. Or similar to Pablo. A representative of the same culture. So I felt vindicated. Or validated. At least for that night. What I really wanted was for Pablo to be there. Watching me get sucked off by another Latino guy. That would've made me come even harder than I did.

So I know what he wants tonight. I know how he feels. It's no fun being rejected. And there's only one fix. That's why I don't think he's going to be here long.

I'm ready. I've got the machete right here with the duct tape. The Glock.

I may not even need the duct tape after all. I can have him lie down on his stomach in the alley. Then use the machete. It may take several blows to cut through his neck. I suspect that's the case. But the first blow should kill him, right? If I sever his spinal chord. That's instant death, isn't it? He can't yell out or struggle if he's dead. So I may not need the duct tape. I'll be killing him instantly. Which in a way is very humane. Compared to what he's done to others.

There's a part of me that *would* like to torture him. I'm at a point right now where in a sense it's tempting. I can see doing things to him in a big protracted way. Like cutting off his dick:

"That's for Reese." Cutting off a finger: "That's for Tuffy." He could lose a lot of body parts. It could take a long time. He's done a lot of sick shit.

I could hack off his foot. "That's for Brice."

But there would be a price to pay for it later. Psychologically. I don't want to risk that corny shtick where I turn into him. I'm not the sadist, he is. I want to keep it that way.

Wow, here's a cute guy. Coming up the sidewalk. Going into the Laundromat with a bag of clothes. A little blond guy in shorts, baggy tank top. Athletic tank top. He's got that hayseed look. Farm boy look. Like Bryan Adams without the acne scars. Boy Scout type. All-American. I'm suspicious though. Of anyone doing their laundry at one-thirty in the morning next to L.A.'s biggest raunch pit. But maybe I'm cynical. Maybe I'm jaded. From living too long in this city.

He's really doing his laundry. Pouring in the Tide. Sticking in the coins now. So maybe I'm sick. Maybe I'm wrong. To think everyone's as sex-obsessed as I am.

He's reading a book now. A young hayseed intellectual. I should go talk to him. Pick him up. It's still not too late to bail out of this.

Except it is. Here comes Pablo. Oh, man. This is it. Here he comes. Alone, as predicted. Dick no doubt sticky in his black jeans. Semihard and sticky with the spit of seven men. He's feeling relieved. Cocky and smug. Good.

OK, I'm ready. As soon as he goes around the corner, I'm out of the car.

Wait a second. Oh, fuck. Oh, no. No, no. He's still walking. But he's seen the blond kid.

Never mind, Pablo. Keeping going. That's it. You just got off, what do you want?

Fuck. He's stopping. He's going back. Back to the Laundromat. He's shambling back.

Now he's looking through the window. The dirty, smeared window. He's checking out the kid. Who's sitting there, reading. He hasn't seen Pablo yet. Or has he? I could've missed something when Pablo walked by the first time. Some exchange.

OK, the kid just looked up. He knows Pablo's watching him. I think he already knew.

Oh, man. I don't like this. Pablo's just standing there now on the sidewalk. Watching blatantly.

Right. The kid just scratched his crotch. Adjusted his cock. He's still pretending to read, but he's getting a hard-on.

Right. He just put one foot up on the chair. So Pablo can see his dick in his shorts leg.

Shit. Pablo's going in.

Pablo's standing in front of him now. Are they talking? I think so. But not much. Pablo's just standing there, letting the kid see the thick swelling shaft in his Levis. I can tell he's got a hard-on just from the way he's standing.

Right. The kid just copped a feel. What's he going to do? Suck Pablo's cock in the Laundromat? It wouldn't surprise me.

But the kid's getting up now. Yeah, he's got a hard-on all right. It's poking out the front of his shorts. What is this? A Laundromat or a pornomat?

OK, now they're definitely talking. Now they're leaving together. What's going on? What about the kid's clothes?

They're walking back up the street now. Back toward the Backfire. Are they going to go in there? Do it in there?

No, they just passed the entrance. Wait a second. I get it. The kid came up on foot. He must live nearby.

OK, they just turned the corner. I've got to see what's going on.

✽ ✽ ✽

Oh, man. I'm pissed. I still don't believe what's happened. I had it, Jim. I had his fucking confession! I had it right here on tape. *Except this fucking piece-of-shit Walkman didn't record it!*

I'm going to check it again right now. To make sure it's even recording *this*.

OK. It seems OK now. So I must've just missed the Record button earlier. I mean, that's clearly what happened. I can see why. I was under duress. I was distracted, having him in the car. Finally having him here. Finally talking to him. After all the shit I've been though.

So I'm at the seashore now. You can probably hear the waves crash. I'm up on a bluff at Palos Verdes. Watching the full moon over the water. It must be three-thirty or four now.

I needed some air after what happened. Some fresh sea air. After the slaughterhouse district stench. That's why I'm sitting here in the grass on the edge of this bluff. To get some fresh air. To try to feel halfway pure again, if that's possible. I don't think it is.

But I want to tell you now about what happened. I need to remember what he said while I can. I need to tell you now because I'm not sure how I feel. If I have the stomach to go through with the rest of this.

I could jump off this bluff and it would kill me, I'm sure of it. It's a thirty-foot drop. Rocks and waves below. Like that shot in *Rebel* after the cars go over. I don't know. It's funny. A part of me wants to do that. This isn't really like I thought it would be.

So anyway, this is what happened. Do I sound numb? Do I sound affectless? Like I'm being affectedly affectless? I don't mean to. I'm not posturing. I'm just exhausted. Physically, I mean.

So anyway, where did I leave off? I can't even think now. I'm completely zoned out. OK, back in Silver Lake. That's right. Way back in Silver Lake. The kid at the Laundromat.

OK, all right. So Pablo leaves with the kid. I wait till they walk around the corner, then I follow. I follow on foot. But when I reach the side street I don't see them. They've disappeared. The street's dead, deserted. Like *The Third Man* in Silver Lake. Like postwar Vienna with palm trees. That kind of feeling. Like where the fuck did they go? Down a manhole?

This side street is industrial. Beat-to-shit buildings, concrete yards with razor-wire fences. Yellow security lights. Nothing that looks like any kind of residence. But I still look around, since I don't see where else they could've gone. But all these places seem closed up tight, dead.

Finally I decide to walk on around the next block. To double back to where Pablo's truck is parked, assuming it's still there, so I can stake it out. I start to hurry, thinking: What if he's left? But I can't figure why they'd take the long away around to the truck.

I'm walking so fast, I almost miss it. I'm walking down this street that has more storefronts and I almost don't notice this blurred shadow on the window. In one of the storefronts where there's a dim light burning back behind the fogged windows. Which could be a security light. But I notice some sort of movement peripherally and almost don't pay attention. Then I stop and think: Did I imagine that or what?

So I go back and I definitely see shadows through the fogged glass. Movements. People moving inside. It's this typical storefront with the glass door set back from the sidewalk between two windows. And everything's fogged so you can't see in. Except in one window I notice a scratch of light. So I look through the scratch.

Inside it's much brighter that I expected. Almost floodlit with warm lights that are somehow strangely flattering. Like the angle of light makes everything look glossy. Pablo's back, for example, looks as smooth as satin. Like a Bruce Weber photograph. Except actually he's sweating.

So is the blond kid. Pablo's got him tied to a post. His hands are tied up above his head. His shirt's already off, so there's this young teen-boy back. Then Pablo pulls down the kid's shorts, so you see his firm little butt. But that's not all you see. You notice this blemish above the kid's right butt check. Or is it a birthmark? Then you see in the bright friendly light that it's purple. That's when you know it's a lesion.

I think that's why I don't do anything for a minute. Except what I'm already doing, which is watching. As Pablo undoes his pants and pulls out his cock. Which I can't see since Pablo's got his back to me. I see his butt though, as his jeans drop to his knees. His sweet brown butt, which is moderately hairy. For a second I wish he were someone else, someone I could save.

I know he's not wearing a rubber. I haven't seen his cock,

171

but I'm positive he's not. So he's fucking this kid without a rubber. And he's looking down, like he enjoys watching his cock slid in and out of the young blond butt hole. He's looking down in the bright light, so he has to see the kid's lesion. So clearly he doesn't care.

Then I think of how I could walk in and fuck him. Fuck Pablo in the ass while he fucks the kid. And I wonder, with a Pablo sandwich between us, if I wouldn't be all right. If I wouldn't be protected. Pablo might be getting HIV right now. He might be contracting it this instant. But it wouldn't reach me. It couldn't move that fast, up his dick, through his organs, to his hot tight asshole. So if I fucked him now, I could shoot before it reached me.

I even think he wouldn't mind. That if he saw me entering, he'd jump at first in shock. Then he'd say, "Yeah, do it. Do it, man. Fuck me. Get it out of your system."

Which almost makes sense. As the attitude he'd take. To imply that I was mad for only one reason. Because I couldn't fuck him anymore.

But I couldn't fuck him now, even if I wanted to. Because I can't get a hard-on. Physically, it's not possible. Because of what they gave me at the hospital. But here's the question I can't answer. If it hadn't been for the drugs in my system, *would* I have had a hard-on? I think the answer is yes. I think in that case I might have stepped in. And held the gun to his head and fucked him.

Instead, I step in with the gun out and Pablo says, "Oh, shit." As he looks over his shoulder and sees me. He jumps and says, "Oh, shit," and pulls out of the blond kid, and he isn't wearing a rubber.

The blond kid looks at me and he isn't what I thought. Up close, he doesn't look like an innocent farm boy. He's sharp-featured with a nasty mouth. He looks like a mean little queen.

He says, "Hey, dude. Private party." Like what does he think? This gun in my hand is a prop or a toy? Like a fetishistic sex trip? How lame can a chewed-up blond boy be?

For a second I think about shooting *him*. That's how much despair I feel. Like this whole scene's a sick joke, a sick parody of something. In a way I'd like to kill them both and throw up. Since I'm not saving anyone. They're both doomed garbage.

But the kid has blue eyes. These big blue eyes. Which triggers something rancidly sentimental. That's the only reason I don't blow his head off. Instead, I start to untie him, but I don't even have to. The rope's not that tight. I tell him, "Get the fuck out of here. This doesn't involve you." I'm not even looking at him. I'm looking at Pablo as the kid ducks out.

Then it's just me and Pablo in the bright storefront. He's just standing there shirtless and sweaty with his cock stuffed back into his half-buttoned jeans. It's so strange to finally be looking at him after all the shit I've been through. To be looking into his scared brown eyes. To realize he's not as big as he seemed in my mind. Or as young. To look at his wet sensuous mouth and still, on some level, just want to kiss him.

He says, "Dean, this is crazy. Do you know how crazy this is?"

I don't know how long I stand there just looking at him. It's like I'm spacing out in some weird way. But then I think about the blond kid, wondering if he's going to alert someone. Which he may or may not. I feel I gave him the impression that Pablo and I were boyfriends. That we were boyfriends and I'd caught Pablo cheating or something. But he could still call the cops anonymously. "There's a man with a gun..." So I say to Pablo, "You're going to come with me now. If you make any trouble, I'll kill you."

I lead him down the dark street, going on around the block, back toward my car. I keep the Glock stuck in his back. I hold him by the arm, which is strange. The warmth of his skin. To actually be touching him again.

It triggers something in me that I don't want to kill, and that I want him to know he hasn't killed. So I tell him, "You know, all I ever wanted to do was love you."

He says, "Dean, you're crazy. You really need help."

I say, "Pablo, that won't work. That worked at one time, but not anymore. I know what you're about now. I know you killed my dog."

He says nothing for a second. Then he sighs and says, "Oh, man. Is that what you think? I didn't kill your dog. If you think that, you're wrong."

I tell him, "Pablo, you don't lie well when you're scared. If I'd had any doubt, you just erased it."

Then we're coming to my car. This is the most dangerous point. I have to unlock the car and get out the duct tape. The street is deserted but you can hear the music coming from the Backfire. Someone could step out at any second. If he's going to bolt or yell for help, this will be the time.

But he doesn't. In fact, he's strangely docile. Like a guy who's been busted, who's about to be handcuffed, knowing resistance is pointless. He's sighing a lot, like he's disgusted but resigned.

I tape his hands behind his back, then push his head down, just like the cops do, and shove him into the backseat. When he sees the machete, he says, "Dean, Jesus." With a tone halfway between compassion and pity. Like he's still trying to make me fill like *I'm* the psycho. He's not giving up on that tack.

I get in behind the wheel and start the engine. That's when I see the blond kid again. Back in the Laundromat. Putting his load in the dryer. This bothers me. Why is the kid so nonchalant? Because he's already called the cops? I get out of there fast and don't start to relax till we're on the freeway.

That's when I start the recorder. Except just as I'm doing it, Pablo thrashes around in the backseat. I think that's what distracted me. That's why I fucked up and didn't hit Record. I look back and he's just trying to sit up. So I wonder if I shouldn't have taped his legs, too. In case he tries to kick me or something. But I can't see why he'd want me to crash on the freeway. With him in the car.

I can't help but notice that he still looks hot. Having his hands taped behind his back really shows off his pecs. He's all sweaty and erotic-looking, and a part of me still wishes that we could be boyfriends. But I know that's part of his sick spell.

He sees the ice chest now, the Rubbermaid Sidekick, and says, "What's in the cooler?"

I say, "Nothing yet."

He sighs and says, "Oh, Dean." Still acting like I'm flipped out or something, psychotically copying a movie.

He says, "You don't need to do this."

I say, "Maybe not. But I'm not taking any chances. I'm going to kill you anyway. What do you care if I cut off your fucking head?"

This is where this strange thing starts to happen. Where I imagine his reply: "You don't have to cut off anyone's head, Dean." And my reply to that: "Why not? You have. You talked about it once in your sleep." This whole exchange, which I suddenly realize is all in my mind. He hasn't even said anything.

That's when I know he's doing something to me. Using his thoughts to fuck with my head. I know that I have to take charge again before he saps me or confuses me further.

So I say, thinking that the recorder's getting all this, "What did you do to Reese?"

He says, "I didn't do anything to Reese."

I say, "You saw him at the sex club, didn't you? On Thursday night."

He says, "Reese was obsessed with me."

I say, "You saw him, didn't you?"

He says, "Yes. But nothing happened."

"What did you say to him?"

"Nothing. I just asked him to please leave me alone. I said, 'What are you doing? It's been four years. Get over me, for God's sake. Get a fucking life.'"

"What else did you say to him?"

"Nothing. He got crazy after that. He broke down. He started sobbing. Clutching at me on his knees, begging me to come back to him. Humiliating himself. Maybe he liked that, I don't know. But it was grotesque. They had to make him leave. I was embarrassed for him."

I say, "No, you weren't. You loved it. That's what you love."

"No, I don't," he says. "I know what you've done, Dean. You've made me a monster in your mind. I'm not perfect,

OK? But I'm not the evil person you think I am."

I say, "You stole animals. You ran a theft operation."

He says, "That's not true. I know who told you that."

I say, "I saw you kill a dog. I saw you stab a dog in the eye, Pablo."

He says, "I don't know what you think you saw. But I've never done anything like that." In a second, he says, "Look, I don't know what happened to your dog."

I say, "Yes, you do. You took him. The same way you took Mark's dog and Reese's cat. You took him and used him in one of your rituals—"

"My what?"

I say, "Pablo, I talked to your landlady. She told me what she found."

"What landlady?"

"Pablo, I know all about your Palo Mayombe shit."

"My *what?*"

"I know you were involved with Adolfo Constanzo."

"Who?"

"Pablo, I know you stole a brain from work. An ex-boyfriend's brain. That's why you got fired."

He says, "That's not true. I didn't steal his fucking brain."

I look back at him. For the first time he's letting some anger show.

I say, "I know you've got all this rationalized. Integrated—"

He says, "You don't know anything."

"—so you don't know how sick you are. How evil."

He says, "You're going to find out what evil is."

I say, "Pablo, you can't hurt me anymore."

He says, "Wanna bet? I know what to say right now that

would drive you insane, even more than you are. That would make you kill yourself right now. You don't know who you're fucking with."

I say, "Yes, I do."

I brace myself for a verbal onslaught, but instead he falls silent. Except for more heavy sighs as we soar through the downtown interchange. It must be three by now. Hardly any traffic. Just the *Dragnet* buildings, the lighted City Hall.

Finally he says, "Look, Dean, I'm sorry. I'm just scared, that's all. I know how mad you are, and I don't blame you. I'm not a good person, I admit it. I have problems. I'm a sex addict."

"I don't care about that."

He says, "I know you came looking for me at SCA. A friend of mine saw you there. I'd been going there myself until then. But I quit because I was afraid of running into you."

"Right. It's my fault that you're a scumbag."

He says, "No, it's not your fault. Don't you see what I'm trying to tell you? It wasn't your fault that it didn't work out with us. I got scared, that's all. I've got intimacy issues."

He's not trying to be funny. But I laugh. Then I say, "Pablo, shut up."

He says, "Look, I've got AIDS."

I say, "I know you've got it *now*. After fucking that kid without a rubber."

He says, "No, I tested positive. Four months ago. My T-cells are already dropping. I'm doomed. I'm paying the price all right, for not sticking with you. What more do you want?"

I say, "I want your fucking head in this ice chest."

He says, "Wouldn't you rather have me die in agony? A slow, horrific AIDS death?"

"Yes," I tell him. "In a perfect world. And when the AIDS quilt came to town, I'd take a giant shit on your square."

He says, "I don't blame you for being angry with me."

We fall silent again. There's just the roar of the freeway. I feel like a cop transporting a prisoner. That's our dynamic. He can try any verbal strategy he wants. But he knows that I know that he's guilty.

On the Santa Ana Freeway, I say, "What did you say to Reese?"

He says, "I told you. Look, Reese was a speed freak. He was fucked up. What he did to himself was bound to happen."

I say, "Pablo, you tried to kill me. You burned down my house in the middle of the night."

He says, "I didn't do that." Then he says, "You assaulted my mother. You're insane, Dean. You're obsessed with me. I think you're psychotic right now."

I say, "You killed my dog, Pablo."

He says, "I didn't kill your fucking dog!"

I say, "You've killed people, too, haven't you?"

He says, "No, I don't do that. I've never done that."

I say, "If I shut off the recorder, will you tell me the truth?"

He says, "There is no truth. There's nothing to tell."

I don't know what else to say. He isn't going to give me anything. He isn't going to give me any kind of satisfaction. To let me know, beyond any doubt, that I'm right.

Except that's when he says, in this kind of bored rush: "All right, I killed your dog. I slit his throat in a ceremony. I had somebody burn down your house. I also killed Mark's dog and Reese's cat. And I've killed lots of people, too. Mostly in

Mexico with what's-his-name. And I was going to kill the blond guy I was fucking. I was going to strangle him, then cut out his heart. So you saved his life. You're a big hero. I've tortured people in Chile. I'll bet Anne told you all about that. I helped Jeffrey Dahmer kill some guys, too. What else? Oh, right, I stole my dead boyfriend's brain and fucked his cadaver in the ass while I was at it. Is that enough? You want more? I know you're going to kill me anyway. Is your conscience clean enough yet?"

He's trying to fuck with my head, of course. But I know that what he's just told me is basically true, except for the thing about Dahmer. I don't say anything. There's nothing more to say. I take the next exit.

I don't know where we are, what city. An industrial area. Norwalk or someplace. Except there's a smell. Fertilizer, animals. A barnyard smell. Like there might be a Farmer John slaughterhouse nearby.

I pass a gas station, keep going, trying to find a dark place. All the buildings have security lights, so I start to get frustrated. Finally I come to another gas station. But this one's boarded up, the pumps removed. No lights. I pull around back.

For some reason I can't look at him now. I say, "I'll be right back. I've got to take a leak."

He doesn't say anything. He's sulking now.

I get out and walk around the side of the building, so he can't see me. I take out the baggie of speed, surprised to see how little is left. I pour what's there out onto my hand and snort it. I wait till it hits. It's not as much as I'd like, as I need, but it's something.

I move, knowing I can't stop to think now. I walk back to

the car, open the door. I say, "Come on, get out."

He sits up. I help him out. He doesn't resist. He's kind of groaning. Going, "Oh, Jeez. Oh, God." Half with dread, half with a strange kind of excitement.

I say, "Lie down on the ground."

He looks at me and says, "Oh, Dean." The way he used to say it when I was fucking him and he was about to come.

He gets down on his knees, but stops there. Presses his chin down to his chest, so that his neck is almost horizontal. "Like this," he says.

And I flash on some photo I saw as a kid. In a World War II book. Of some formal Japanese prisoner-beheading scene. Where the prisoner is kneeling just like this, the executioner with his sword raised. And I realize that's the way Pablo wants it to be. Like a ritual. Since he is this total ritual queen.

I get the machete out of the car. If he'd wanted to bolt, he could've done it then. But when I turn back to him, he's still on his knees like a supplicant.

I hesitate and he says, "I'm ready, Dean."

For a second I don't know what's going on anymore. This is not the way I pictured it. I expected him to fight me, not to say, "I'm ready." His brown back is so glossy in the moonlight. I want to touch him. I want to stop all this and hold him. Like some big cathartic moment of tenderness in a liberal-humanist nonviolent film. Where we'd both say "I love you" with tears on our cheeks.

Then he says, "Come on, *do it.*" In a much tougher voice. He used to say the same thing, in the same voice, when I was fucking him.

But I'm spacing out. My mind doesn't want to be there. So it takes me a second to hear what else he's saying. That he's doing what is almost a sexual incantation. But instead of saying, "Yeah, fuck me, Dean," he's saying, "Your stupid fucking gringo dog. I slit his fucking throat. But first I cut off his paws. I cut off his stupid fucking paws. And watched him bang around, howling and bleeding—"

That's when I do it.

It takes more than one blow to cut off his head. I guess I cut through his spinal chord with the first blow. But he's still alive and kind of groaning as he pitches forward on the asphalt. Then I just keep at it, a whole bunch of times. I mean, I cut his head completely off with five or six blows or something. But I don't stop there. I'm pretty much gone. Like a frenzy type of thing. Hacking at his body, his torso, which is now just a carcass anyway, a dead piece of meat. I guess it's kind of hard to stop it. Or there's no point or something. You've crossed the line, you're doing it. So you might as well get it all out of your system.

Afterward I feel funny. Not sorry I've done it. But lonely somehow. Sad that he's no longer there. If that makes any sense. Because I feel that we've done this together. That's what I see now. That he wanted me to kill him.

And for a second I'm suspicious about that. Feeling that even at the end he was somehow in charge. That he'd manipulated me. Like he knew I'd see that, that it would piss me off afterward. Knowing he had the last laugh or something.

But mostly I wish it had just been a game or something. A dream or a movie. That he could get up and say, "That was wild." I still wish we could get up and laugh and go to New Mexico, win Nobel Prizes. Except that isn't possible, had never been possible. Since Pablo couldn't laugh.

So his head is in the ice chest now. Sitting on the shotgun seat. That's why I'm out on the bluff. I know it's just his head and his brain can't still be working. But it doesn't feel safe in the car anymore.

I'm not sorry about this. But I'll be glad when it's over.

I guess I'm going to go ahead with the rest of it. I don't see any reason not to now. I owe it to the others, if not to myself. To have these curses lifted now.

I can see how that works now. I see Hugo's point. How just killing Pablo doesn't solve everything.

Maybe magic works even if you don't believe it. It might be like electricity. You can not believe in it all you want and still get fried.

✢   ✢   ✢

I'm back on the freeway now. Heading south into Orange County. The sun's coming up. Pink sky ahead. I'm going down to San Juan Capistrano. To meet Hugo at the mission there. I guess he knows someone. A priest or a padre or whatever the fuck they call themselves there. Some fag Catholic priest maybe. Something like that. I don't know much about Catholicism really. Since I was raised as a Methodist. I mean, I don't know about its secret workings. I have to trust Hugo, that he knows what he's doing.

I don't know much about Capistrano either. I've never been there. I don't even know when the swallows come back. They could be there right now for all I know. There could birds all over everything. Singing that song, "When the Swallows Come Back to Capistrano." All swaying in unison like birds in a Disney cartoon.

TAPE 6

Hey, Jim. At long last the completion.

I'm glad that you finally got the other tapes. Sorry it cost you like that, but that's the way things work down here. *El soborno* [bribery]. It's no secret.

I still have mixed feelings about your book idea, to be honest. That's why I don't want to see the transcripts. I might freak out. Not that I don't remember what I said, kind of. But if I actually saw it in black and white, and thought about everyone reading it, especially now, when so many people hate me, I don't know how I'd feel.

At the same time I want the whole thing to be known. It still pisses me off the way the Taco Bell thing overshadowed everything else, so that that's all I'll ever be remembered for. Not that I don't understand, from a media standpoint. But it still seems homophobic. If I were straight, if I'd had a problem with an ex-*girl*friend, they'd go all into it. They'd want to do a TV movie or something. With Mark Harmon as me or something. But because it was a guy, they don't want to go into it. It's also racist, too, since Pablo was Latino. They just say, "Seagrave was angry. First he killed his ex-boyfriend, cut off his head." That's almost always all they say. Like I'm a psycho, which pisses me off. They don't even want to deal with the rest of it.

Sometimes I think Pablo's magic's still working. That he put the fear into Ed Bradley. Did I tell you about that? He was going to come down and talk to me for *60 Minutes*. Then nothing. Like maybe someone killed his dog. I'm not being facetious either, incidentally. I know Pablo had accomplices who are still out there. Palo Mayombe is still alive and well. That's one of the reasons I feel safer here.

I'm trying to think back now to that morning in Capistrano. I guess I can now without getting too upset. In a way, it's a good thing it's been six months. I've only talked about it one other time, incidentally. To Arturo. Because he understands. I talked about it some in Tijuana. Right after my arrest. Just enough to get the results I wanted. 'Cause I could see where things were going. How the feds were going to take it. The G-men, I mean, who were trying to take me back. They thought I was faking. So I could cop an insanity plea. But the Federales got very spooked when I mentioned Palo Mayombe. I mean, if they were dogs, their fur would've stood up. They take that shit *very* seriously down here.

But let's go back to Capistrano. Yes, I remember driving down the San Diego Freeway. It's late morning at this point, and the sun is directly in front of me. You think you're driving south, but it's actually east. So the sun's right in my face. And I can't find my dark glasses.

By this time I'm ragged. I'm still tweaked but exhausted. My adrenal glands must look like sucked-dry prunes. I'm kind of short-circuiting or something maybe. Because I'm talking to myself like a homeless person. Like some sidewalk schizophrenic. I try to stop doing it, but I can't. I feel this pressure. Like if I don't let it out, my head will explode.

Except I'm not exactly talking to myself. I'm talking to Pablo. As if he were there in the shotgun seat instead of just his head in the cooler. Saying things I wished I'd said while he was living. So in a weird sort of way it's almost therapeutic. Like one of those therapy things where you talk to a pillow that's supposed to be your father or someone.

So I'm saying all these things I would never want anyone to hear, least of all Pablo. Since he would make fun of me, use it against me. The same way other people would.

I'm saying things like, "I only wanted to love you. I wanted to live the rest of my life with you. Does that make me crazy?"

I say, "Why were you so evil? What did you get out of it? What was in it for you? I still don't get it. When you could've had so much more by not being evil."

I say, "You've ruined my life now, whatever else happens. I'm going to have to leave the country now. I'll never explain this. I'll never convince people I had to do this. You set me up, didn't you? You were going to die anyway, if it's true you had AIDS. But I don't even know if that's true. You're such a fucking liar, Pablo. You're a pathological liar. You should have gone to Liars Anonymous."

That's when he says, "I warned you, Dean. I told you the first night that I was no good. But you didn't listen."

I say, "I know. I let my cock lead the way. And paid a steep price."

He says, "The sex was good. I wasn't lying about that. Remember how I used to come when you fucked me? That's not something you can fake."

"I know," I tell him. "It was *too* good, Pablo. That's what drove me insane."

He says, "You said it, not me."

It feels good that he's responding. It's comforting, but I don't take it seriously. My mind is like a city with the sound turned up. It's just a voice I'm choosing to focus on. And I like it being so effortless. Not something I'm thinking up, but a voice that has its own life, like something in a dream.

Then he says, "I want a cigarette."

I laugh and say, "What are you going to do with that? Your lungs are back in Norwalk, my friend."

He says, "Come on. I haven't had a smoke since Silver Lake. I'm having a nicotine fit."

By now I'm feeling that his voice is coming from the cooler. But I know it's aural illusion. The cooler seems to be humming, though. Almost like it's electric. Except I decide the whole car is. It's just the engine vibration. I remind myself I'm tweaked.

He says, "Come on. I'll even settle for one of your shitty Kents."

For the first time I think about looking in the cooler. Thinking that will stop it, if I look at his head. But I'm afraid to do it. I say, "Pablo, forget it. No cigarette."

He says, "Darn. I want *something* in my mouth. Maybe not a cigarette. Maybe something big and hard and juicy."

This is starting to bother me. I say, "Pablo, just shut up, OK? Stop trying to fuck with my head."

He says, "I'm not trying to fuck with yours. I'm saying I wouldn't mind it if you fucked with mine. I wouldn't mind seeing that big gringo dick in my face."

"You'd like that, wouldn't you?" I tell him. "I've been pure up to now. You'd love to turn me into a fucking necrophiliac."

"That's just a label," he says. "It might be a rare treat."

"It's sick, Pablo."

"Nobody's watching. Everything's permitted."

"It's not happening."

"Choirboy. Pussy."

"I'd do it if I *wanted* to, Pablo. But I don't *want* to. It doesn't sound appealing."

"You sure *used* to like to. Dean, the face-fucker. Face-fucker Dean."

"That was then, this is now."

"I could lick your balls, too. I know you like that."

"Knock it off," I tell him. "Just can it, OK?"

He starts moaning. "Oh, yeah! I want that cock in my face! Right in my face, man! Just like the old days."

That's when I shove in the Jesus and Mary Chain cassette. Crank it up to drown him out. Which seems to work. At first I still hear him moaning. Then I'm not sure. Then it goes away. So it's all right. It's finally stopped. Like a car alarm that was driving you crazy but is finally truly off.

I keep the music up loud, though, just to be certain. Till I reach the San Juan Capistrano turnoff. As I'm coming down onto the surface street, some commercial boulevard, the music ends and he starts in again.

He says, "Dean?" in this timid, apologetic voice.

I sigh, like I'm his father or something. "What?"

"I'm sorry. I was out of line. About you fucking my face, I mean."

"That's OK," I tell him. "Let's forget it."

He says, "I know how hard this whole thing is for you, Dean. You're a good person. I don't want to torment you. Or make you do anything you'd feel bad about later."

I'm looking for the mission. I have no idea where it is. It could be anywhere, even along this trashy boulevard, between the fast food places.

I say, "Pablo, I know what you're trying to do. This is your last chance to fuck me up before your head goes into the *nganga*. Because that's where it going to go. You can try any trick in the book, but nothing's going to dissuade me."

That's when he says, "I want a burrito."

Which I *know* is a memory. I can still see him saying the same thing at the counter at Tito's in Culver City. I have it on film in my mind.

He says, "Come on, I'm hungry. I want a burrito. Why don't you stop at this Taco Bell up here?"

I can't help smiling. Because I've got him, he just blew it. How could he know there's a Taco Bell up ahead with his eyes in the fucking cooler? Can he see through white plastic? I don't think so. I say, "OK, Pablo. I'm hungry, too, as a matter of fact. One burrito coming right up. You want all-bean or meat-and-bean—

"Combination," he says.

"Anything to drink?"

"A large Pepsi," he says.

There's no drive-through window and the lot looks full, so I park on the street. I get out and walk up. I have no intention of buying a burrito for a severed head, but I do need some coffee. And I need to ask directions to the mission.

I'm kind of shocked when I walk in and see how crowded it is. I mean, it's a mob scene, which means I'm going to have to wait, which I don't like. I don't like the people either. Typical Orange County breeders. Except there's a funny kind of energy that makes me think of something religious. That's when I notice they all seem to be together, talking loud, with overbright, zealous eyes. So I think it must be a church group or something. It's Sunday morning. Then I notice a dork in an Operation Rescue T-shirt. I see a few placards: DON'T KILL YOUR BABY, shit like that. Like there's some kind of rally or protest nearby.

I catch a few people checking me out. Like I'm a weirdo, not with them, but I'm defiant. Fuck you, right-wing slime. You can fire any evil shit at me you want, I'm staying here till I get my coffee. That's my feeling.

Then I hear somebody behind me say my name. Which I still think happened, OK? I heard the name *Dean,* which is not that uncommon. So I'm willing to accept that maybe they weren't talking about me.

But at the time it bothers me. Especially when I look back and see these two Christian girls doing this number. Obviously looking away from me real fast, then giggling. Looking at each other with this mean, conspiratorial giggle. I don't think I imagined this. Probably they just thought I was weird, but it sets something off inside me. I want to kill them, that's the feeling. And suddenly I feel like everyone there is thinking about me. Like they're aware there's this stranger there, one who is not of them, and they're all thinking hateful, judgmental thoughts. Which I think may be true. I'm willing to say I shouldn't have cared. I shouldn't have been so sensitive. But I was, so I had to get out of there.

But when I reach the car I suddenly stop on the sidewalk in this state of indecision. I know what's going to happen if I get back inside the car. I know it's not real, but I'm still going to hear it: "Where's my burrito?"

So I stand there a minute beside the car, trying to decide how to deal with all this. I look back at the Taco Bell and at first I think the people are still watching me. Laughing at me, like they know I'm a coward, like they scared me away. Then I decide they're not. That I'm just being paranoid. Like I have this moment of clarity. So I decide to go back in and use the john, to take a leak and wash up, which I had thought of doing anyway, since I'm totally grunged-out. I decide to just act normal, to ignore any other feelings. So I unlock the trunk and take out my satchel, so that I can change into fresh pants and a clean shirt.

I go back in, but the men's room is occupied. That's where the problem starts, because while I'm waiting I see these same two girls again, and this time they're definitely talking about me. I still don't think I imagined that. Cutting them some slack, I probably looked insane.

Finally this pudgy guy comes out of the men's room, and I go in and lock the door. That's where I really cross the line, I guess. For starters, it smells like shit, like the pudgy guy just took a dump, and there's no ventilation, no windows. Just these white walls and fluorescent lights that are flickering. I try not to breathe so I won't smell the stink as I wash my hands and face. Then they aren't any paper towels, so I have to use toilet paper.

Then I open the satchel and take out a T-shirt and along with my clothes there's the Glock. And I look at the gun and start to hear these voices telling me to blow off my own head.

At first I think I'm imagining it. Then I realize the voices are coming from the people outside. Not literally, like they're whispering through the door. But telepathically. It's the kind of thing where if you looked at them you might not see it. They might be talking and laughing with another Christian. While at the same time sending out these hateful messages. "You're shit, you're worthless, you're a sick queer, spare the world. Kill yourself, just do it, you'll never know love." But it's all so subtle you almost think these are *your* thoughts. Which, of course, is what they want you to think. They want you to interiorize this shit, so you'll do it.

So I start to see it as coming down to them or me. That's what it feels like. That without really wanting it, I'm in this moment of truth where I have to go one way or another. I can be a pussy, a coward, and let them have their way. But that goes against everything I am. I haven't come this far to curl up my toes and grease myself under pressure from some vile Christian fucks. So I pick up the Glock, which is loaded, and get ready. I have two extra clips, seventeen rounds each, which I know I'm going to need. I stick the clips in my back pocket.

I wish I could tell you that it was fucked up or something.

I feel some pressure to say that. Like: Oh, it was horrible, I felt really bad afterward, don't do this, kids. But that's not true. It was ecstatic. That's the big secret about killing people. Although I guess everybody secretly knows it anyway. At least certain kinds of killing. I don't mean cold sadistic torture. Pablo's kind of killing. To me, that's another thing. That's sick. But when there's real passion involved, or anger, there's a kind of ecstatic release.

I can still see the whole thing in slow motion. I shoot the girls first, the two who were laughing at me. They go sprawling like rag dolls that hardly weigh anything. Then I just keep firing. *If they move, kill 'em.* And they're moving, so I do. Hitting anyone and everyone. A serious right-wing turkey shoot.

One guy who looks like Charlton Heston does this big exploding brain shtick. Most people just go sprawling. There's this big sense of messy awkwardness.

The Glock's a bitchin' gun. I can see why they're so popular. Just enough recoil to make the shooting experience pleasingly visceral—without knocking your hand off the way a .357 does. A loud, crisp, definitive bang. *Satisfying.* That's the right word. Like eating something crunchy, a bag of tortilla chips.

In some ways the screams are the best part. Just like in films when there's gunfire in public. The women screaming and whimpering. The way they scream at the sight of Clint Eastwood's big steel horse cock. The way they whimper when it's over, when Steve McQueen steps around the bloodied body in the *Bullitt* airport. For some reason those female sounds mark a pleasing sense of closure. A tasty dip for the crunchy chips. Black bean or spicy guacamole.

In the end I only go through two clips. Because the place empties quickly, except for the wounded and dead. I don't know what I expected. That they'd just stand there like dumbstruck targets and take it? But it seems to be over much sooner than I'd like.

So I make it to the car. Nobody tries to stop me. They're all scattering every which way. A real sense of panic in the street.

What else can I tell you? Do I regret it? Oh, sure, in a way. But I now think it was something that just had to happen. They caught me at a bad time, and I don't mean that glibly. I think those people hated me. Or would have, if they'd known who I was. Those were the people who rejoice that AIDS is killing queers. I just picked up on their hate at a time when my brain didn't have a filter.

I admit I was lucky. If I'd killed twelve handicapped children, instead of twelve evil hard-right Christian zealots, I don't know what tune I'd be whistling today.

At this point, of course, making my appointment with Hugo at the mission was out of the question.

The part I do feel bad about is what happened at the border. Even though that really was not my fault. In another way, though, if it hadn't happened, I'd probably be in a California state hospital now or in a cell next to Charles Manson.

Because I wasn't really planning to run the border. I still had this sense that if I was cool enough I could slip across in the Sunday foot crowd. I knew they'd be watching for my car, so I even took the long way, going inland instead of taking I-5. I tried to look at the Thomas Guide, but I was too tweaked to make sense of it. It's a miracle that somehow I knew which way was south.

I was around San Diego somewhere when I got rid of Pablo's head. I realized I had to. It was starting in again. It was making fun of me. Like it had set me up one more time, knowing what would happen if I stopped for that burrito. I knew it was bullshit, but I couldn't take it anymore. So I opened the passenger door and flipped up the cooler lid and dumped the head out without looking at it. I was still afraid I might see the eyes or the mouth moving or something.

For a second I thought I heard it laugh. Pablo's wet shriek. Which I'd only heard two other times. On the tape when he stabbed the collie in the eye and in the theater at the Bette Midler trailer. I thought that's what it was till I heard it again and looked in the rearview mirror. It was this Latina maid sitting on a bus bench, watching Pablo's head roll into the gutter. I'm still not sure if she was laughing or screaming or both.

I'm glad I didn't kill anyone at the border, although at the time I thought I had. What else could I think?

I come around the corner, doing maybe sixty, and suddenly there are a half dozen people running right at my car! Put yourself in my place. Can you imagine how that feels? It's worse than a nightmare. Especially when you've been through as much as I had and think you're almost home free.

It's a crazy thing to do. It's crazy and desperate, and I feel for those people on a human level, to want to get across the border that bad. But it's also insane, to count on gringo cars all stopping. Or maybe most gringos don't want to go the other way as badly as I did.

I didn't even have a chance to hit the brakes. The second I saw them, they were going *boom, boom* against the hood of the car. Add another *boom*. I hit three of them in all. Two guys and a woman. I'm glad they survived. But that's when I floored it. What else could I do?

I knew it was over. But I wasn't thinking. I just had to keep going. It was that kind of thing. So I crashed through the barricade, but I had no illusions. That I would disappear into Mexico at that point or anything.

I'm surprised I got as far as I did. Before I crashed into the school bus in Tijuana. I'm glad it was empty. I would've felt like shit if I'd killed any kids.

You know the rest. In fact, you know more than I do about the U.S. coverage. I've seen the stuff on CNN, but we don't get the American tabloid shows here. I've heard about them though. That's why I won't talk to them. They've already categorized me.

What you don't know about is Arturo. I'm hesitating now because there's a chance he may hear this. He'll be mad if I say too much, but I'll take that risk, since in a way he's very hot when he gets angry. He's very Latino that way. Unlike Pablo, who was dark-skinned but emotionally Swedish. And no matter how mad Arturo gets, I don't think he'll really hurt me. Unlike Pablo, who never got mad but hurt me a lot. Also—and I know you're going to think I'm cracked or something—but Arturo looks a lot like Andy Garcia. I know what you're thinking, I've got some star fixation or something. But I don't. It's just a fact. If you ever meet him, you'll see what I mean.

When I first met Arturo I was skeptical. Just the term *Mexican psychiatrist* filled me with foreboding. Let's face it, Mexican medicine doesn't have a good rep. If you were going to get a face-lift and wanted to make sure you didn't end up looking like a gargoyle, would you go to Guadalajara? I don't think so. So I thought: What is this guy going to want to do to me? Put me in an ice bath? Give me a lobotomy?

But Arturo's cool. In fact, he went to Yale and he's incredibly sensitive and brilliant. Plus he comes from a powerful Mexican family that has all these different connections. That's what saved me. You know how bad the feds wanted me back. But Arturo made a phone call and said, "They'll never touch you."

By then we'd talked a lot and I knew I could trust him because he understands what happened to me. He worked closely with Omar, Constanzo's femmy boyfriend, after his sentencing back in 1990. Before Omar died of AIDS. So he knows all about Palo Mayombe. He's an expert on the different ways that it works. That makes him controversial and even feared by some people, since a lot of Latinos believe in it literally. I don't think Arturo does. But he respects its power. He thinks that I got sucked into it.

"With your mind you knew it was bullshit," he said. "But with your heart you believed."

Another time he said that Pablo had "sexually beguiled" me. At this point it's hard to dispute that.

The truth is, sometimes Arturo sexually beguiles me. Not that we've fucked or anything. He's supposedly straight. Not that he's said so. He's been very professional. His private life hasn't come up. But I know he's single. Thirty-six and single. So what do you think? A guy who looks that good has got to be fucking someone. And I'll bet it's not a woman.

Besides, I can tell he's in love with me. He'll shit if he hears this, since I don't think he's ready to admit it yet. How can you blame him? I'm this patient in a maximum security hospital with an undetermined sentence. So I'm not exactly boyfriend material.

In a way, there's no rush. I'm still putting myself back together. Arturo got me a room in the special ward, which is not plush but comfortable. It's not a cell. He got me drawing materials, which I haven't used yet. But I know that I will and soon. I'm getting some ideas that I don't want to rush. Ideas that are fresh, untainted.

I'm still HIV-negative, by the way. Arturo had some blood tests run last week. Not that I was surprised. About being negative. Except I had some question, in case Pablo really had it. Wondering if maybe he'd had it all along. But I'm OK.

And I found out another thing. I've got too much testosterone. I asked Arturo, "What's too much?" He said, "When you do the things you did, that's too much." Which he meant as a joke, and we kind of laughed about it. He *can* laugh, which is another cool thing. I could tell it also turned him on a little. That I'm a *joto* but *muy macho* with two fat *cojones*. I've noticed the same thing a few other times. Like when he asks about my sexual history. Do I like to fuck, that kind of thing. Not that he puts it quite that way. He uses clinical jargon. Like "anally passive," and stuff like that. And he's not voyeuristic or anything. It's not like he's sitting there jacking off while I talk. But once he got embarrassed when I told him about my favorite kind of sex, which is do it for hours, you know, fool around for hours, sucking cock and so on, without coming, till you're both transported to another euphoric world.

James Robert Baker

    I'm on three different drugs, which thank God are not like Thorazine. I don't feel like a zombie, but I'm not anxious. Another drug I took for a while gave me dry mouth, so Arturo changed it.

    I think I know what's going to happen. After everything dies down, in a year or two, he'll release me. He can do that anytime he wants. I respect him for not coming on to me, for having such rigorous ethics. But once I'm a free man and no longer his patient... Well, I'll put it like this. It's something to look forward to. The first time we kiss deeply and take our clothes off in his tropical bedroom in Cuernavaca. So there's this sweet sense of anticipation. That's what I'm living in now, in this kind of dreamy state. Looking forward to the shock of first contact. The smooth warmth of his brown skin.